MEET THE GIRL

Sabrina Wells is petite, with curly auburn hair, sparkling hazel eyes, and a bubbly personality. Sabrina loves magazines, shopping, sleepovers, and most of all, she loves talking to her best friends.

Katie Campbell is a straight-A student and super athlete. With her blond hair, blue eyes, and matching clothes, she's everyone's idea of Little Miss Perfect. But Katie has a few surprises for everyone, including herself!

Randy Zak has just moved to Acorn Falls from New York City, and is she ever cool! With her radical spiked haircut and her hip New York clothes, Randy teaches everyone just how much fun it is to be different.

Allison Cloud is a Native American Indian. Allison's supersmart and really beautiful. But she has one major problem: She's thirteen years old, five foot seven, and still growing!

PROBLEM DAD

By L. E. Blair

GIRL TALK® series created by Western Publishing Company, Inc.

Western Publishing Company, Inc., Racine, Wisconsin 53404

©1991 Western Publishing Company, Inc. All rights reserved. Printed in the U.S.A. No part of this book may be reproduced or copied in any form without written permission from the publisher. All trademarks are the property of Western Publishing Company, Inc. Story concept by Angel Entertainment, Inc. Library of Congress Catalog Card Number: 91-75730 ISBN: 0-307-22022-2   R MCMXCIII

Text by Katherine Applegate

Chapter One

"First you slice him open very carefully. Then you reach in and pull out his heart," Allison Cloud, one of my best friends, calmly explained.

Allison was sprawled out on my big old cast-iron bed. I was sitting on the floor, along with Sabrina Wells and Katie Campbell, my other best friends. It was Thursday afternoon after school. On Friday during science lab we were going to dissect frogs to study their anatomy. That's why we were all hanging out in my bedroom. We were supposed to be memorizing the anatomy of a frog, but we were doing a whole lot more talking than memorizing.

Of course, Al and Katie were taking the whole thing a lot more seriously than Sabs and I. Those two really get into school, even when they're not there. If you ask me, it's some kind of genetic thing. I just didn't inherit the homework gene. I inherited the music gene. I'm like my mom, more the creative type.

"The great thing is, we'll get to see all his internal organs," Al continued.

"Psych!" I exclaimed. "I get first crack at the knife, Al!"

"You two are disgusting!" Sabrina wrinkled her nose. "Some poor innocent little frog is going to die at our hands, and you're actually looking forward to it!"

"It's all in the name of science, Sabs," I replied with a grin.

"What you have to understand, Sabs," Allison explained, "is that dissection is the best way to understand anatomy. A frog's system is a lot like a human's."

"Too bad for the frogs, huh?" I joked.

It's great having Al for a science lab partner. Allison's incredibly smart and loves to read. She's like a walking encyclopedia. A mind reader, too. Next to my mom and Sheck, a guy who's my best friend back in New York, Al knows me better than anyone on the planet.

On top of being really smart, Al's also really beautiful. She's a Native American, a real Chippewa Indian, with a kind of exotic look.

She's very tall and graceful, with long, thick black hair, the type of girl who really stands out in a crowd. She was even offered a modeling contract with *Belle Magazine* once.

"I still say it's unfair to the frogs," Sabs argued. She shook her head, sending her thick auburn curls flying. She and Al couldn't be more different if they tried. To begin with, Al's five foot seven and still growing. Sabs barely makes five feet, even on her tiptoes. And Al's very quiet and a little shy. But "shy" is definitely not a word you'd ever use to describe Sabs. She knows everybody and everything, and she can talk a mile a minute.

"The point is," Sabs continued, "if I wanted to be grossed out, I'd rent one of Randy's warped horror movies at the video store."

I laughed. Everyone knows I love a good horror flick — especially a good *bad* horror movie. The dumber the better, I always say.

"Allison's right, Sabs," Katie said. "Besides, the frogs will already be dead by the time we get to them." Count on Katie to see the practical side of things. She's always very logical.

"I'm going to try to create Frankenfrog," I said. "I'll collect all the leftover parts —"

"Stop it, Randy!" Sabs cried, but she had this grin on her face, and I knew she was only half as grossed out as she pretended to be. I can't help teasing Sabs because she takes it so well.

"You know, all this talk about frog guts is making me hungry," I said. "How about a munchie break?"

"But we still have the whole muscular system to learn," Katie pointed out.

Too late. Sabs and I were already halfway downstairs. A minute later Katie and Al joined us in the kitchen.

My bedroom is in a loft right above the kitchen — perfect for sudden attacks of the munchies. I guess I should explain. My mom and I live in a barn. That's right, a barn. When you look at it, it's hard to believe that horses and pigs used to live here. When my mother and I moved here after my parents' divorce, she had it totally converted. Now it's just perfect for my mom and me.

She's an artist, and she uses the right half of the barn as a studio. The huge skylights in the ceiling give her plenty of light. And since I'm a musician, having a loft to myself is great for practicing — especially since I play the drums.

4

I'm the drummer for a band called Iron Wombat, and when I'm practicing and I really start pumping, it's a major miracle the roof stays on.

I started to microwave some popcorn. "Hey," Sabrina asked, peering into the living room, "where's Olivia, anyway?"

My mom likes my friends to call her by her first name, but Sabs is the only one who can manage to say it without practically choking. Technically, my mom isn't really "Mrs. Zak" anymore, since she and my dad are divorced. I've called Mom "M," and Dad "D," for as long as I can remember.

I'd be willing to bet you major bucks that I'm the only person in Acorn Falls, Minnesota, who calls her mother anything other than "Mom" or "Mother," but hey, I'm used to being different. When we moved out here from New York City at the beginning of the school year, it took a while for me to adjust to everyone at Bradley Junior High — and for them to adjust to me.

"M was in her bedroom, last I saw," I told Sabs. M's bedroom is next to the kitchen, on the other side of the barn, and it's walled off by big

Chinese screens.

"I love that new painting on the easel in the corner," Katie said. She adjusted the sky-blue ribbon holding back her straight blond hair. It perfectly matched her blue-and-white-striped turtleneck. Katie's what you might call a preppie dresser. She wears lots of sweaters and matching cardigans and stuff. She's the all-American girl-next-door type. I'm definitely not the girl next door, not unless you live in New York City. I practically live in black. As far as I'm concerned, the day you catch me wearing something pastel, you can have me committed, because I will definitely have gone into permanent brain lock.

While we waited for the popcorn, Sabs headed into the living room and turned on the TV. She grabbed the remote and zipped through the dial. Usually when we get together to watch TV, we try to hide the remote control from Sabs. I can relate, though. I get bored pretty easily myself.

"Hey, flip back a channel," I called, just as the popcorn started popping in the microwave. "That was one of D's commercials, I think."

My dad lives in New York City and produces TV commercials and music videos. It's definitely a cool job, except for one thing — it keeps him incredibly busy. That means I don't get to see him as often as I would like. Hardly ever, in fact. We talk on the phone a lot, though. Usually he's on his car phone. Half the time the connection's lousy, and he's usually on his way to an important meeting or something, but he does try to take five minutes to shoot the breeze with me. Well, *almost* always.

We gathered around the TV just in time to catch the end of the commercial. A tall blond girl wearing a pair of jeans and a red silk blouse was leaning over the side of this seriously impressive yacht. "Cubex Jeans," she cooed. "More than cool —" Just then a huge wave caught her right in the face.

The commercial is part of a whole series D is shooting. They always start out dead serious, with a gorgeous model in some beautiful setting. Just as she's telling you how cool she and her jeans are, something funny happens that catches you totally by surprise.

"I love the one where the skater lands on her rear on the ice," Katie said. "I can definitely relate to that!" Katie quit the flag girl squad at the beginning of the year so that she could try out for the boys' ice hockey team. Not only did she make it, but she became the second-highest scorer on the team. That's what I like about Katie. She's full of surprises.

Just then M walked out of her bedroom. She was dressed to the max in black leather stirrup pants, a white cowl-neck sweater, and a fake-fur swing jacket in a black-and-white pony print. I had to do a quick double-take. I mean, when she'd walked into her bedroom twenty minutes earlier, she was covered with so much paint she looked like she was ready to be framed and hung on the wall. Now she looked totally cool. She could easily have passed for my older sister.

My mom is kind of young. She dropped out of art school when she was only twenty to marry my dad. When people see us together, they sometimes mistake us for sisters because we look so much alike. She's got my dark eyes (or should I say I've got hers?), and her hair's jet-black like mine and just as wild (I wear mine spiked on top and longer in the back). A lot of times we even share the same clothes.

"Hey, haven't I seen that jacket somewhere before?" I teased.

"You said I could borrow it, Ran," M replied, smiling. "Remember the deal? I can borrow the jacket if I let you borrow the pants."

"I wish I could borrow clothes from my mom," Allison said as she pulled out the hot bag of popcorn from the microwave. I laughed.

"Why can't you, Al?" I asked. "Now that your mom has had the baby, she's wearing regular clothes again, right?" Allison's mom had a baby a couple of weeks ago. Al has a new baby sister named Barrett. Allison got to name her, and she named her after her favorite poet, Elizabeth Barrett Browning.

"Oh, it's not that." Allison laughed. "I'm just taller than my mom. She wears petite, but I like her clothes, though."

"Well, you look amazing, Olivia!" Sabs exclaimed.

"Really, you look great," Katie agreed.

"What's the occasion, anyway, M?" I asked. "You don't look like you're on your way to the grocery store."

"Maybe there's some hunk who works there," Sabs suggested, winking at my mom.

M pretended to look embarrassed. "Well, there is that guy in the fish department. You know — the one with the beer belly and the whale tattoo?"

We all laughed. "Seriously, M, what gives?" I asked as I helped Al pour the popcorn into bowls.

"Can't a woman dress up a little without getting the third degree?" M asked lightly, but her voice told me she had something on her mind. She grabbed a handful of popcorn. "Ran, I do need to talk to you for a sec, okay?"

"Shoot," I said.

M nodded toward her bedroom. "Privately, I mean."

Al glanced up. "You know," she said quickly, "it's pretty late. Maybe we should get going, guys."

"But the popcorn!" Sabs protested.

"Really, girls, that's not necessary," M said. "I just need a few minutes alone with Randy."

I wasn't sure I liked the sound of M's voice. Something major had to be cooking for her to make a big production like this.

"We'll just go grab our books," Al said, herding Sabs toward the stairway. That's Al, like I said. She has this sixth sense about things. I knew she could tell that my mom needed more than a couple of minutes to talk to me.

My friends gathered up their books, and I walked everybody to the front door. "Catch you later," I said, waving good-bye. I shut the door behind me and turned to face M. "So, what's the big deal?" I asked.

She sat down on one of the antique love seats in the living room and motioned to me to join her. M really loves antiques. She says she prefers furniture with a story to tell. D's apartment in New York — which used to be *our* apartment — is strictly modern. Lots of leather and chrome. He loves it, and so does his girlfriend, Leighton. But I guess it's just one of many things my mom and he never really saw eye to eye on.

"Listen, Ran," M began, "I'm really sorry I didn't bring this up sooner. It all just happened so suddenly —"

"What happened so suddenly?" I demanded.

M smiled. "Sorry. I guess I should start at the beginning. I was out around lunchtime today, picking up some dry cleaning — remember that shirt I got linseed oil on? By the way, it's not going to come out, not in our lifetime —"

11

"M!" I cried. "Would you get to the point?" M's usually like me — when she's got something to say, she says it.

M ignored me and continued with her story. "So, anyway, I'm standing there in line, and all of a sudden I hear this male voice going, 'Olivia? Olivia Harper?'"

Harper was my mom's name before she married D. "So it was somebody you knew growing up here, huh?"

M nodded. "His name's Terry Murphy. I didn't know him very well. He was two grades ahead of me, and I had a major crush on him in high school."

I laughed. It's kind of hard to imagine your own mother having a major crush on anybody — other than your dad, that is. It's also weird to now live in the same town that my mother grew up in. She's always running into people she used to know from junior high and high school.

"It turns out Terry's a history teacher at the high school," M continued. She pursed her lips and looked away. I had this sudden sinking feeling I didn't want to hear what she was going to say next.

"Well, we started talking, and when I mentioned I'm an artist, Terry told me about a lecture at the art museum in Minneapolis tonight on postmodernism."

I stared at her blankly. I believe my jaw may have been hanging about halfway down to my knees, but I couldn't guarantee it. "You're going on a date?" I asked. "An actual date?"

M laughed. "I know you think I'm past my prime, Ran, but I do have a few good years left before I start playing shuffleboard and storing my teeth in a glass at night." She touched my shoulder gently. "It's just an evening with an old friend, hon. Nothing more, nothing less."

"Hey, you have a perfect right to date, M," I said quickly. "I mean, after all, you're divorced, right? You can't sit around the barn forever like some withered-up old maid."

"Your concern is touching," M teased.

"No, I mean it. It's just that . . ." I paused. "I guess I hadn't really imagined what it would be like, you know?"

"I understand. I'm not sure I had, either." She sighed. "Let's face it. I've been out of circulation for a long time!"

"But you look really hot!" I exclaimed. I cast her my best concerned-parent look. "So what time should I expect you in, young lady? And who is this Terry fellow? I should check him out. You know — make sure he's worthy of you."

Outside, a car pulled up. "That's him," M said. She ran to the window and peeked outside, chewing on her lower lip.

I couldn't believe it. She was actually nervous. I mean, M's never nervous. She's always totally in control, no matter what.

"I'm really anxious for you to meet him," M said. "Just keep an open mind, okay?" she added, using one of my favorite sayings.

"Don't I always?"

As she headed for the door, the phone rang. "I'll grab it," I volunteered, heading for the kitchen.

I picked up the receiver. "Talk to me," I said distractedly, my eyes glued to the door.

"Ran, it's D."

"D!" I exclaimed. It was crazy, but I suddenly felt awkward. I mean, here was my father on the phone while my mom was about to head out on a date with another guy. I knew they were divorced, and I knew D had been seeing Leighton for ages, but it still seemed unreal. Like something out of a bad sitcom.

My mom pulled open the door to reveal this tall, Joe Average kind of dude. I mean he was okay-looking and everything, he just wasn't slick-looking like D — you know, Hollywood. He was wearing wire-rimmed glasses, faded jeans, a plaid flannel shirt, and some worn-out Nikes. He looked, well, like a history teacher.

"It's D," I called to my mom. "Have a good time!"

Terry waved at me, so I waved back, and he and my mom headed out the door.

"Sorry, D," I said. "I had to pause for station identification."

"Was that your mom on the way out?"

"Yeah," I answered vaguely. "Some art thing. You know. So what's up?"

"Big news, Ran. Are you sitting down?"

"Standing, but I can handle it. Trust me." At least, I hoped I could handle it. I took a deep breath and waited to hear what my dad had to say.

One thing was for sure. He couldn't surprise me any more than my mom just did.

Chapter Two

"So, do you want to hear my good news first, or my bad news?" I asked as I approached a table in the cafeteria the next day.

"Better start with the bad," Al advised, pulling out a chair.

Sabs dropped into a chair next to Al. "No, do the good," she argued. "It'll be more fun."

"I think I'll wait until Katie gets here," I said. "Then I can tell you all at once. I was trying to get your attention during homeroom, but you guys were so busy listening to the announcements, I couldn't get a word in edgewise."

Honestly, I don't pay much attention to announcements. I figure if there's something important going on (which, take my word for it, is rare), Sabs or Al will always clue me in.

I opened my lunch bag and pulled out my blueberry yogurt and the pita-and-cheese sandwich I'd slapped together that morning. It was some kind of weird cheese — goat or yak or buffalo or something. M got really carried away at the health food store the other day.

Katie arrived at the table carrying her lunch tray. "Another U.F.O. for hot lunch," she said with a groan. "Unidentifiable Food Object."

"It looks like frog legs to me," I said matter-of-factly. Then I smiled at Sabs. "They have to do *something* with them, after all."

Sabs rolled her eyes. "I swear I'm skipping science this afternoon."

"So what's your news, Randy?" Al asked.

I broke into a smile. "D's coming here to visit!"

"Randy, that's awesome!" Sabs exclaimed. "When's he getting here?"

"Next week." As I said it, I realized that I didn't quite believe it myself.

"But that's not all!" I continued. "You'll never guess *why* he's coming to visit Acorn Falls — besides wanting to see me, of course. I'll give you a hint. It's not for the Acorn Falls nightlife."

"Is he moving here?" Sabs ventured.

"No way, Sabs," Katie said as she ripped open a bag of potato chips. "Somehow I can't see Mr. Zak producing music videos in Acorn Falls."

"Well, how about commercials? Uh, make that *one* commercial?" I said, grinning.

"Ohmygosh! He's going to shoot a commercial here? In Acorn Falls?" Sabs cried, nearly choking on her carrot stick. "This is the most awesome, most amazing, most excellent news!"

"It's great news, Randy. You must be so happy," Al said.

I had to admit I was feeling very pleased. I took a bite of my pita sandwich and made a mental note to stick to Cheddar cheese in the future. "*And* D made me promise to invite you all to the filming. He's doing another Cubex Jeans commercial."

"This will do wonders for my career!" Sabs declared. "I can see how a real live commercial is filmed."

Sabs wants to be an actress someday. I really think she'll make it big. She stole the show playing Frenchy in the Bradley Junior High production of *Grease*. She's got great comic timing. Plus, she's a born ham.

"I know what you mean, Sabs," I told her. "I'm hoping to pick up some video techniques from D. I've really gotten into my photography course lately." A couple of months ago when I mentioned the course to D, he had sent me an awesome camera and video camcorder.

"Maybe I could even be an extra," Sabs said hopefully. "I'd love to be one of those people who stand around in the background trying to look happy and popular. It could be the start of my TV career."

"They usually have only one girl in those jeans commercials, Sabs," Katie pointed out gently. "But maybe you could talk Randy's dad into using you as an extra."

Sabs looked even more excited. "Yeah, and if I can't be an extra, well, then, I could be the water girl. Or maybe I could help the makeup person or something. After all, I know the producer."

"We'll definitely ask D if he can use you," I promised. "Hey, he had one other major piece of news. He broke up with Leighton."

"How come?" Al asked. "They've been together more than a year, haven't they?"

I took a swig out of my milk carton. "All D said was that they were going their separate ways. I have to admit I wasn't exactly brokenhearted to hear the news."

It's not like I hated Leighton or anything. I mean, I didn't know her well enough to hate her. She's young and pretty and blond, but sort of a bingo brain, if you ask me. The kind of girl whose I.Q. matches her bra size.

"You don't suppose —" Sabs began. She stopped herself and shook her head so hard her curls nearly went into orbit. "Never mind," she added, glancing at me, then concentrating on her sandwich.

I was pretty sure I knew what she'd been about to say. "You were thinking maybe M and D could get back together now, weren't you?" I asked.

"Well, it would be so romantic," Sabs said with a sigh. "I mean, your dad will be here visiting, and who knows? One thing might lead to another. Anything could happen."

To tell the truth, ever since D's call last night, I'd been thinking the same thing. After we'd hung up, I'd headed straight for my drums and really cut loose for a while. That's what I always do when I need to think — that, or go skateboarding.

Anyway, the more I thought about it, the

more it made sense. D breaks up with Leighton, and suddenly he wants to come to Acorn Falls. I knew he said he needed a scenic place with a lot of snow, but he could have filmed in places a little more happening, like Aspen or Vail. Don't get me wrong: I really like Acorn Falls now, but I'd be lying if I said this is the kind of town that really jams. I mean, the biggest social event in Acorn Falls is the annual Loon Festival. (That's the state bird, in case you're interested.)

So all the signs were there. But last night when M got home from the art lecture and I told her about D coming, I didn't get the feeling she saw the big picture as clearly as I did. She was glad D was coming to visit, but mostly because she knows how much I miss him, I think. Also, she's anxious for him to see how well she's done on her own since their divorce.

"You know, Randy," Sabs said, shaking me loose from my thoughts, "this could mean two weddings in one year! First Katie's mom, and now maybe yours!"

"What's wrong, Randy?" Al asked.

"M went on a date last night," I muttered.

"No wonder she was so dressed up!" Katie exclaimed.

Sabs nodded. "So that's why she needed to talk to you. Who was the guy?" Her face crumpled. "Not that fish guy!"

"I think Randy's mom was just kidding, Sabs," Katie said, smiling.

I tossed the remains of my pita sandwich into my lunch bag. "I think I would have preferred the beer-belly dude," I said. "This guy had boring written all over him. We're talking boring with a capital *B*, guys. He's a history teacher at the high school. Enough said?"

"Did your mom have a good time with him?" Al asked.

I shrugged. "She said he was really nice. That's about it."

Katie gave me a knowing smile. "That's just how it started with my mom and Jean-Paul."

"What's his name?" Sabs asked. "I'll have to ask my brothers about him."

"Ask them what?" asked Sam, Sabrina's twin brother, as he sauntered up and straddled a chair next to her. His best friends, Nick and Jason, were with him, as usual.

With Sam and Sabs sitting side by side, you could really see the resemblance. They have the same dark red hair and freckles, not to mention the same megawatt grin. "So ask away," Sam said.

"When I say 'brother,' I don't always mean you," Sabs said, rolling her eyes. "Don't forget I have four brothers to choose from." Sabs is the youngest of five kids, and the only girl. They tease her like crazy, but I think she kind of likes the attention.

Me, I prefer being an only child. It just feels right, my mom and I together as a family, you know? For a second I tried to imagine M and D and me, back together again, but the image fuzzed out like a bad TV picture. After all, where would we live? M and I wanted to stay here. (A while back, I would have given anything to leave, but now I think of Acorn Falls as home. Which, believe me, still freaks me out sometimes.) And D couldn't exactly run his business from here.

Oh, well. My mind was getting all fogged up with details. I hate that. I like things to be nice and simple.

The point was, M and I made a good family, just the two of us. But maybe with M and D back together again, we could be a serious team.

Chapter Three

"Yo, Spike!" I called, cupping my hands around my mouth. "Over here! I need to ask you something!"

Al, Sabs, Katie, and I were camped out at our usual table at Fitzie's the following Thursday afternoon. Everybody in junior high hangs out at Fitzie's soda shop after school. Today, for some reason, it was even more packed than usual. I had to call Spike two more times before he heard me.

Finally Spike waved and began making his way through the crowd. When he got to our table, Sabs slid over to make room for him.

"Can't stay." Spike shook his head apologetically. "I've got to get over to the station to inventory the record library."

Spike's a D.J. at KTOP 1350, the student station at the high school, where he has a show. He's in ninth grade, so we go to different schools, but I see him a lot because he lives

24

down the street from me, and our moms are good friends. He's a really cool guy who just happens to be really cool-looking, too, with wild brown hair and jet-black eyes.

"Listen," I said casually, "I was just wondering if you knew this guy over at the high school —"

"Hey," Spike said with a laugh, "I know everybody."

"This is a teacher, though." I concentrated on the basket of fries Al and I were sharing. "His name's Murphy. Terry Murphy. He teaches history."

"Say no more," Spike replied. "I've got Murph for U.S. history this year."

"Murph?" Sabs echoed.

"Yeah." Spike nodded. "Everybody calls him that. He's a cool guy. Kind of laid back, you know, but with a great sense of humor."

"Is he a good teacher?" I asked.

"I'll tell you how good Murph is." Spike reached over and stole one of my fries. "Today we were talking about the War of 1812, and I actually managed to stay awake for the entire period."

"Wow," Sabs exclaimed, "he must be good!"

"What's so boring about the War of 1812?" Al demanded. "I read a book about it last summer, and I really got into it."

"You're right, Al. The War of 1812 was actually kind of cool. Lots of spy stuff going on."

"Hey, Spike," Sabs interrupted. "My brother Luke told me the same thing about Terry Murphy." Sabs took a superbig bite of her hot fudge sundae. "He said Murph's the best teacher he's ever had, even though his essay tests are killers."

"You know Murph, Ran?" Spike asked.

"In a way." I really didn't feel like getting into the whole thing about his date with my mom. I guess I'd kind of been hoping Spike would tell me Terry Murphy was the absolute cellar when it came to teachers. Instead, I ended up with rave reviews about how he's Superteach. Anyway, just because he was a decent teacher didn't mean he was potential boyfriend material for M. I figured I owed it to M to check up on him. Someone had to look out for her, now that D was out of the picture.

D wouldn't be out of the picture for much longer, though, I reminded myself. He was supposed to arrive in Minneapolis late that night.

It was hard for me to believe that a whole week had gone by since he'd first told me he was coming to Acorn Falls. Every time I thought about it, I got so excited I could hardly sit still.

"Earth to Ran," Spike said as he swiped another handful of fries.

"Sorry," I apologized. "I've been spacing all day."

"She's got a good excuse," Sabs pointed out. "Her dad's coming here tonight. He's going to be shooting a commercial in Acorn Falls."

"Ran, that's awesome!" Spike exclaimed.

I nodded. "I'm really psyched."

Spike glanced at his watch. "Hey, I gotta jam. Have fun with your dad, Ran. Maybe you could stop by the station later and give him the grand tour."

"That'd be great. I will, if there's time. Knowing D, he'll have every minute planned." I smiled. "And thanks for the scoop on Murphy."

Spike turned to leave, but he'd only gone a few feet when he collided head-on with Arizonna, who was dashing toward our table at high speed.

"Spike, man. Sorry, dude," Arizonna said

breathlessly. He brushed his long blond bangs out of his eyes. Arizonna moved here from Los Angeles not long ago. He's a total surfer dude, really different from anyone here in Acorn Falls. Which makes him a lot like me, when you get right down to it.

Arizonna pointed to the front window, where a crowd of people was gathering. "I guess I wasn't, like, watching where I was going, 'cause I was checking out this most excellent white stretch limo parked outside."

Spike craned his neck. "That's pretty classy for the crowd here."

"Babes," Arizonna called. "Check out the limo parked out front. It's like straight out of Hollywood."

"Zone, did you see who was inside?" I asked, barely able to control my excitement.

"No way. It's like a mob scene out there."

I leaped out of my seat. It just had to be D. Why else would a limo be cruising through the center of Acorn Falls?

"Come on, guys," I said, leading the way through the crowd. "I have a feeling this limo may be for us."

"In your dreams, Rowena."

As soon as I heard my real name, I didn't even bother to turn around. I knew it had to be Stacy Hansen, no doubt with her clones — Eva Malone, Laurel Spencer, and B. Z. Latimer. I am not what you would call a big fan of Stacy's. Her father's the principal at Bradley, and I guess she thinks that makes her royalty or something. Normally I would have come up with some zinger to get Stacy worked up, but I had more important things on my mind at the moment.

We paid our check at the cashier and finally made it to the door. The long, sleek limo was parked at the curb. A lot of the Fitzie's crowd, plus some people on the street, had gathered around to check it out.

Arizonna whistled. "What'd I tell you, babes? Major wheels."

I took a step closer and tried to peer through the dark windows. Suddenly the back window eased halfway down.

"Need a lift?" a man's voice asked.

"D!" I cried. I spun around and waved to Katie, Al, and Sabs. They were standing on the sidewalk with their mouths half-open. Apparently they'd all forgotten how to talk, because the only reply I got was a little shriek from Sabs.

I reached for the back-door handle, but D held up a warning finger. "Hey," he said, "let's do this right." He nodded to the driver, who leaped out of the front seat and dashed over to the door.

The driver was dressed in full uniform, complete with brass buttons and a shiny chauffeur's cap. "Ms. Zak?" he asked with a bow.

"In the flesh." I nodded behind me. "My friends will be joining me," I said, doing my best imitation of Stacy at her snootiest.

He swung open the door and I hopped onto the white leather seat next to D. He wrapped his arm around me. "Randy, honey, you look fabulous," he said. "You're really growing up."

"You don't look too bad yourself," I said. And he didn't. D could have stepped out of the pages of *GQ* — that's this men's fashion magazine. Compared to him, the male population in Acorn Falls looked like a bunch of hicks. To begin with, D has this ponytail, which, trust me, looks really awesome on the right kind of guy. He's got one pierced ear, where he wears this small diamond stud. And he's always decked out in designer suits.

Not that D's a snob or anything. But he always says if you want to *be* your best, then go ahead and *look* your best.

When you're a producer, looking good is very important. D's always doing lunch and making deals with all kinds of superrich types. Wearing designer labels kind of goes with the territory. M used to joke that she always felt like a frump next to D. That's crazy, of course, because M could look hot in her painting shirt and a pair of sweatpants. Secretly, I think it's just that M was never into the whole glamorous scene the way D is.

"This is so cool!" Sabs cried as she hopped into the limo and sat down across from us. "Look, there's Stacy. I bet she's having a major cow!"

Al and Katie piled in right behind her, and the driver closed the door.

"Sabs, Al, and Katie," I said, "meet D."

"Please, call me Peter," D said.

"Don't count on it, D," I replied with a laugh. "M's still trying to get everybody to use her first name."

D pushed a button on a shiny wooden panel, and the glass partition separating us from the front seat lowered.

"Ran, why don't you give Paul here directions home?" D said.

"Sure. But first I have to say good-bye to someone." I stuck my head out the window and waved to Stacy. "It's the only way to travel, Stace!" I yelled.

I wouldn't normally make a big deal out of the limo and everything — I mean, in New York City, you see them practically as often as cabs — but I couldn't resist giving Stacy a hard time. As I closed the window, I could see she was still trying to come up with a good retort. Stacy may have guys fawning all over her, but she's not very quick on her feet, if you get my drift.

I gave Paul directions to Sabs's house, since it came first, then turned around to face D. "So, how'd you find me, anyway?" I asked. "I thought you weren't getting in until late."

"I wrapped up some loose ends ahead of schedule and caught an earlier flight. When I got into town, I called your mother, and she said I'd probably find you at Fritzie's."

"*Fitzie's*," I corrected. "Not exactly Le Cirque, eh?" That's this restaurant in New York City that's definitely not your typical Acorn Falls kind of hangout. Put it this way: They don't serve french fries and chili dogs.

D shrugged. "Acorn Falls has a certain charm," he said, but I had the feeling he was just trying to be nice. "I can see why you and your mother like it so well," he added. "How's she doing, anyway?"

"Great," I said. "She's got another gallery show coming up in Minneapolis soon."

D nodded, and his eyes had a kind of far-away look. "I've really missed you both," he said quietly.

Sabs caught my eye and gave me a little wink. I knew she was already thinking about being a maid of honor at my parents' remar-riage. I wasn't quite that far gone, but I had to admit there was definitely a sentimental tone in D's voice.

"You know, you could practically live in this limo!" Al exclaimed, gazing at all the gadgets.

"All the conveniences of home," D said. "There's even a VCR."

"I'm definitely getting one of these for prom night," Sabs vowed.

"You'd better start saving now," Al teased.

D stared at Al and crossed his arms over his

chest. "Are you in seventh grade, also? What was your name? Al?"

"It's Allison, actually," I answered for Al, since she looked kind of uncomfortable. "We just call her Al for short."

"And my name's actually Sabrina," Sabs chimed in.

"Well, I have to say I never dreamed I'd be in the company of such a gorgeous group of ladies," D said. "You're all planning on coming to the commercial shoot, I hope!"

"Are you kidding?" Sabs cried. "We wouldn't miss it for the world!"

"I've already got people here scouting for locations, and we'll probably start filming —" The phone rang and D rolled his eyes. "Duty calls," he said. "Excuse me for just a moment. It's probably my production people in New York. We're having some last-minute casting snags. Just give me five."

He picked up the phone and immediately began rattling off orders. Suddenly I realized how familiar it all seemed — me sitting there, listening to my father on the phone. That was pretty much how I thought of D — always in motion, and always working.

I knew I'd have to share him with his work while he was visiting, but that was okay. I was plenty used to that. The important thing was that he was actually, finally, really here in Acorn Falls. And pretty soon he'd be seeing M. There was no telling what could happen next. Like Sabs had said, anything was possible.

Chapter Four

After we dropped everybody off, I gave Paul directions to our barn. "What do you think?" I asked D as we drove up.

He shook his head, chuckling under his breath.

"Well?" I prompted.

"It's, uh, very rustic," he offered.

"Wait'll you see inside. There's ten times the space of your apartment in New York City."

"Any pets I should know about?" D asked, arching a brow. "You know, dogs, cats, or cows."

"Just Elsie," I answered with a laugh. "We keep her in the kitchen so we won't have to go so far for milk." The limo rolled to a stop, and I leaped outside.

"Thanks for the lift, Paul," I said.

He smiled and gave me a little tip of his cap. "Anytime, Ms. Zak."

"I'll just be a few minutes, Paul," D said. As D stepped out of the car, I glanced over at the front door and just about freaked. Terry Murphy was standing on our front porch! For a nanosecond I actually considered shoving D back in the car and telling Paul to hit the road, but fortunately, some small part of my brain was still functioning.

"Who's that?" D asked.

I shrugged. "The mailman?" I ventured. Let me make this clear. I didn't exactly lie. I just took a wrong guess. I mean, it's not like me to lie. I never can see the point in it. Just tell the truth and get on with life, I figure. But at that particular moment, I really thought it would be in everybody's best interest to get Terry out of the picture. I figured if I stalled D long enough, Terry would climb into the aging puke-green Dodge Dart in the driveway without anybody having to be introduced to anybody else.

"So, Paul," I said, lingering by his window, "what've they got under the hood of this sucker?"

Paul looked at me in awe. I guess he wasn't used to girls asking questions about engines.

"Well, it's one of the biggest V8 engines they make." I think he was grateful for the conversation. Being a chauffeur must get kind of lonely. "Wanna take a look?"

D touched me on the shoulder. "Maybe we should save the engine tour for another time, Ran," he said. He waved to my mom, and she waved back. Terry was halfway down the steps, but he didn't look like he was in any hurry to get a move on.

"It's just that I've never seen a really big V8 engine before." Which was true. Of course, I hadn't wanted to. I'm not exactly into cars. As far as I'm concerned, skateboards are the only civilized way to travel.

"Well, I'm going to say hello to your mother," D said, striding up the driveway. I gave Paul an apologetic shrug.

"I'll have to take a rain check," I said. I headed across the yard, hanging back just a little so I could see what would happen next.

"Olivia," D said as he climbed the porch steps. He gave my mom a long hug. I watched carefully for signs of anything significant. But as P.D.A.s went (that stands for "public displays of affection"), it was pretty standard stuff. I checked out Terry's reaction, too, but it was hard to tell what he was feeling. He looked pretty neutral, but then, he has one of those neutral sorts of faces.

"Minnesota must agree with you," D said to my mom. "You still look beautiful." He took a step backward and cocked his head, still holding on to her hands. "You've done something new with your hair, haven't you?"

"Actually, yes. I've been working on a painting all day, and I've got about a dozen shades of acrylic paint in it by now," she joked.

D let go of my mom's hands and shot Terry a questioning look. "So I understand you're the mailman?"

I decided that this was a particularly good moment for me to drop to the ground and retie my sneakers. To tell the truth, they didn't need it, but you can't be too careful.

Terry laughed good-naturedly. "Terry Murphy." He reached over to shake D's hand. "Actually, I'm a history teacher at the high school," he added as he pushed up his glasses with his index finger. "If I were with the postal service, I'd probably be making enough to replace my junkmobile over there."

"Terry's an old friend of mine, Peter," M added. She turned to Terry. "This is Peter Zak, Terry, my ex-husband."

D winced. "That 'ex' sounds like a movie rating, Liv. There's got to be a better way to describe your devoted husband of twelve years."

M laughed. "Hey, I can think of plenty of words to describe you, Peter, but I'm not sure you'll like them any better."

That's the way M and D always used to talk to each other, bantering and joking around a lot. I'd almost forgotten what a big part of my life that used to be.

"Randy?" M called. "Come on over here, will ya? I want you to meet Terry."

I'd run out of laces to tie, so I knew I couldn't delay meeting Terry forever. At least now I had D around for moral support. I walked over and smiled. A polite but bored-with-the-whole-thing smile. At least, that's what I was aiming for.

"Ran, this is Terry Murphy, hon," M said.

"How's it going?" I asked. "Sorry I couldn't say hello the other night, but I was on the phone with my dad." As soon as the words were out of my mouth, I realized I'd just let it out of the bag that M and Terry had gone out on a date. I scanned D's face for a reaction, but he seemed more interested in checking out our barn.

"Manny tells me you're a member of Iron Wombat," Terry said, smiling at me. Manny is the nickname of Mr. McManus, the music teacher over at the high school. I'd met him when I was helping Spike out at the radio station.

"He said he's caught your act over at the Roadhouse and that you're really good," Terry added.

"Maybe the band could come over some night and jam a little while you're here, D," I suggested. I'd sent D tapes of our gigs at the Roadhouse before, but it wasn't the same as being up close and personal.

"I'd like to hear you guys, if there's time," D replied, sneaking a quick glance at his Rolex. D's always checking his watch, because he's always late for something or other.

"Have you been playing a long time, Randy?" Terry asked.

"I bought Ran her first set of drums when she was six years old," D answered for me. "She was driving us insane, banging with a pair of pencils on every flat surface in the house."

Terry grinned. "Every parent's nightmare."

I was beginning to feel a little left out of the conversation. D and Terry were actually getting along. Maybe D didn't get the fact that Terry and M were kind of an item. More likely, he just didn't see Terry as a rival. After all, there was no comparison.

I looked at the two of them standing there side by side and shook my head. What could M possibly see in Terry, a guy who probably thought an exciting evening was bowling a couple of games at Lois Lane's and having a Smoothee at the Dairy Queen? No, Terry was definitely not in my dad's league. But then, not many guys were.

After a few minutes Terry left. D decided to take a quick tour of the barn. As usual, he moved through the house like a cyclone. I think the tour only took about three minutes. Before I knew it, he was out the door and headed back to his hotel.

But before I even had the chance to miss him, he called and invited M and me to dinner. M decided to pass. I think it was so D and I could have some quality time together. I tried to convince her to come along, but she kept talking about how she had this painting she really wanted to finish.

When I told him M couldn't make it, D suggested I ask Al, Sabs, and Katie along. Of course, they were all totally psyched about going. It took a while to convince everyone's parents to let us go out on a school night. After all, it was Thursday night. As far as I was concerned, the weekend had started. But then I suggested the old "it'll be educational" routine and they fell for it. Works like a charm every time.

We tied up the phones for the next hour trying to decide what to wear. After tearing my closet to shreds, I finally decided to talk M into letting me borrow the outfit she'd worn on her date with Terry. She pretty much had to say yes, since the jacket was mine.

After D had picked everyone up in the limo, he announced that he was in the mood for Japanese food. Acorn Falls isn't exactly the fine-dining center of North America or anything, so we ended up driving all the way to Minneapolis.

Actually, Paul did the driving. We all sat in the back of the limo and watched music videos on the VCR. D had a whole selection, and he played D.J., mixing videos he had directed with others that he just thought were cool. Sabs was going absolutely nuts. She couldn't really believe she was riding around with someone who had actually hung out with half of her favorite stars.

"Did you ever do a video for Paula Abdul?" Sabs asked.

She was going down a list of every rock group or performer she could think of. It was getting to be a very long list.

"No," D answered. He grinned when he saw Sabs's disappointed look. "But we did meet at a party once" — he paused for a dramatic moment, giving me a wink — "at the Boss's place."

"*The* . . . the Boss?" Sabs echoed. "You mean Bruce . . .?"

D nodded nonchalantly. "Springsteen. Great party. Great food. And I made some good contacts." I had to struggle to keep from breaking up. It was so obvious that D was trying to make a good impression on my friends, which was really cool of him. Not that he had to try very hard. Maybe he was doing too good a job, because when he said "Springsteen," Sabs actually stopped breathing. Katie leaned over and passed her hand back and forth in front of Sabs's face.

"I think Sabs has gone into a celebrity coma," she said. Al cast me a look.

"Maybe we should talk about something else, Ran," Allison said, laughing. "Otherwise your dad might accidentally say 'Bon Jovi,' and then Sabs would be lost for good."

"Very funny," Sabs said good-naturedly, snapping out of her daydream. Like I said before, Sabs is easy to tease, but she always takes it really well. "As though I would get all excited just because your Dad had met Jon Bon Jovi. I'm not some hick, you know." Sabs sniffed and stuck her nose up in the air.

Everyone was quiet for about a minute. We knew Sabs couldn't resist. Finally she turned to D, her eyes wide.

"So, Peter," she said, doing her best to sound casual, "not that I care or anything, but have you ever met Jon Bon Jovi?" Which cracked us all up, even D.

When we finally reached the Japanese

restaurant, D led us right to the sushi bar. We sat down together, and he asked the Japanese chef behind the counter to give us each a small sampler plate.

The chef was amazingly fast as he sliced up a bunch of different fish. He wrapped some of it in seaweed, and put other pieces on top of little balls of rice. Then he arranged everything very artistically on small black lacquer plates.

When he placed a plate in front of Katie, she cast me this nervous look — the kind people in the hot-lunch line at school get on meat loaf days.

"Um, Ran?" she whispered. "Shouldn't one of us mention to him that he forgot to cook this stuff?"

I shook my head. "I don't want to embarrass the poor guy," I said. "Let's just eat up." I picked up a piece of the sushi, some raw sea bass over a thin green layer of seaweed that was wrapped around a ball of rice. "I guess I'll just eat mine raw."

Then I popped the fish in my mouth. Katie's jaw was hanging down so far, I could count all of her lower teeth. I couldn't help laughing.

"It's sushi," D explained with a smile. "You

eat it raw, just the way it is." He demonstrated by lifting a pink piece of salmon sushi and popping it in his mouth.

"See?" he asked Katie. "Nothing to it." One by one, Al and Sabs and Katie tried the sushi, and one by one they got this relieved look on their faces when they realized they weren't going to keel over and die or anything.

"I guess now we're all ready for New York City," Al joked.

"Eating sushi is definitely one of the requirements," I agreed.

"Funny you should mention New York, Allison," D said, glancing at Al. "I was thinking that New York City could be a part of your future someday." Al looked confused, but I couldn't blame her. I wasn't quite sure what D was getting at, either.

"It's just that you have an unusual look, Allison," D explained. "Unusual as in good, not unusual strange," he added. "And modeling agencies are always looking for a face that stands out."

"Al was offered a modeling contract with *Belle Magazine*," Sabs said as she reached for another piece of salmon.

"I'm not surprised," D said. He was staring at Al with this kind of detached gaze I recognized right away as his "professional" expression. He got it a lot. Back in the city, we'd be walking along a crowded street, and all of a sudden D would dash off and grab some perfect stranger who had just the right look for one of his commercials. Or we'd be driving along, and he'd suddenly stop in the middle of an intersection and create a mega traffic jam, just because he'd discovered the ultimate setting for his next video.

D poured himself a cup of tea out of the black pot in the middle of the table. "So what happened with the *Belle* offer?"

"Well, I did one layout for them," Al answered. "But when they offered me the contract, I decided I just wanted to be a normal person for a while, if you know what I mean." She glanced down at her plate and gave a little shrug. "It's sort of hard to explain."

D smiled, and nodded his head. "I know exactly what you mean. Plenty of time for all that when you get a little older. Still . . ." D looked over at me and winked. "One little modeling job right here in Minnesota wouldn't be too much to handle, would it?"

"One job?" Al repeated.

"Truth is, Allison, I'm having some trouble lining up a model for the Cubex shoot." D sighed. "I thought we were all squared away, but then the girl we had signed got the mumps. She'll be fine, but it's an outdoor shoot, and with the cold and all . . . Anyway, we need a young model to fill in, and I think you'd be perfect."

"Al!" Sabs squealed. "That would be so incredibly cool!"

In spite of her excitement, I could tell that Sabs was just a little disappointed D hadn't picked her. Sabs can never hide what she's feeling, even for a second. Her face is like a wide-screen TV of emotions. But it was obvious she was really happy for Al, too. For some reason I wasn't feeling quite so generous.

Sure, I could see how Al would be perfect for the commercial. And it wasn't like D was saying he liked her better than me, or anything, because that's just the way commercials are. Directors are always trying to find a person with a certain "look." Sometimes the "look" they need is someone frumpy, or old. But for

Cubex Jeans, Al was absolutely right.

I'd been staring down at my plate while I thought all this through, and when I looked up, I saw Al gazing at me thoughtfully. "Could I think it over, Mr. Zak?" she asked politely.

"Well, don't take too long, okay?" D said. "I need to know by the end of tomorrow." He paused for a minute. "I suppose you're too young to be thinking about college and all. . . ."

Katie and Sabs both laughed. "Peter," Sabs said, "Al has been thinking about college since she was in kindergarten!"

It was practically the truth. Al was the only student in seventh grade who actually had college catalogs sent to her.

"Well, it's just that the job would pay a thousand dollars," D explained. "It'd be a nice addition to your college savings, Al. You have to flip a lot of burgers to make a thousand bucks."

I could see Al was considering. After all, with a new baby in the Cloud family, that kind of money would come in awfully handy when college rolled around.

"Well, I still have to talk it over with my parents," Allison began.

"Do it, Al," I interrupted. "You'd be perfect

for it. Really."

Al looked at me again and I nodded. I mean, Al is my best friend in the world (except maybe for Sheck, who's a guy, so it's a little different). And besides, that little twinge of jealousy, or whatever it was, had already passed. I wasn't about to stand in her way. Al broke into a wide smile. "All right, then," she said. "I'll do it! I'm sure I can convince my parents to let me be in the commercial."

"Then it's settled," D proclaimed. He has this way of just announcing things like they're done deals.

"Spectacular!" D continued. He patted me on the back. "Who would think I'd find my Cubex girl right here in Acorn Falls. Aren't things working out great, Ran?"

"Couldn't be better," I said. I don't think I sounded very convincing, but nobody seemed to notice.

Chapter Five

D spent most of the ride home from Minneapolis talking on the phone. By the time we'd dropped Al, Katie, and Sabs off, he was still yakking away — something to do with a guy in Los Angeles named Richie.

Paul pulled the limo up in front of our barn, and I started to get out. I figured D would be tied up for a while longer. But just as I reached for the door handle, D grabbed my arm.

"I gotta go," D said into the phone, looking at me. "Yeah, Richie, there's somebody more important than you I have to talk to." D listened for a moment and grinned. "Yes, Richie, as a matter of fact, it *is* a beautiful young woman."

I think I may have almost blushed, which is not something I normally let myself do. D hung up the phone and sighed. "Sorry about all that, Ran. I wanted to spend the evening with you, and instead I ended up spending half the time glued to the phone." He shrugged. "And before that, I was busy trying to hire one of your friends."

"That's cool, D," I said quickly. "Business is business." It's one of D's favorite sayings.

D gave me this kind of wistful look. "That should be 'Business is just business.' And business is not as important as my one and only daughter."

I didn't exactly know what to say. D and I have never been real big on major emotional displays. But I could see he was serious. And I have to admit, it was nice to hear.

"Listen, Ran. I know you probably have a busy schedule, but I was wondering if you could make time to hang out with me tomorrow after school."

I broke into a grin. "I'll have to check my social calendar, but I think I can probably squeeze you in."

"You could show me around Acorn Falls," D suggested.

"That would take only about ten minutes," I said, laughing. "You've already met about half the kids at my school."

"Hey, I have an idea," D said suddenly. "You

must have a record store in town. What if I take you shopping? I've been hearing all kinds of great new groups, and I could point out some good stuff you might like."

"I am definitely good to go on that," I said eagerly.

"Spectacular. How about we pick you up right after school."

"Around three-fifteen would be good," I answered and started to get out, but before I could open the door, Paul was there to do it for me.

"Thanks for dinner, D," I said.

"Hey, I'm the one who should be thanking you," D said. "It was a gas."

As I watched D's limo pull away, I was feeling totally jazzed. I'd really been a fool to get worked up over D paying more attention to Al than to me. The night had turned out okay, after all. And tomorrow was going to be even better.

I really was lucky. After all, how many other dads could take their daughters shopping for tunes and actually know which music was really happening?

Friday morning I woke up a few minutes before the alarm went off. That was definitely one for the *Guinness Book of World Records*, since I am *not* what you would call a morning person. I have this big old-fashioned alarm clock with two brass bells on top. When it goes off, it's loud enough to wake somebody in a coma, but somehow I usually manage to sleep through it just fine.

So there I was, my eyes wide open, with a whole two minutes to go before the alarm was supposed to blow. A minor miracle. I guess I was kind of excited, looking forward to the day and all. Actually, it wasn't the school day I was looking forward to. We had a science quiz on frog anatomy scheduled that I wasn't too thrilled about. But the end of the day, when D was going to pick me up at school — now, that was something to get fired up about.

I rolled out of bed and let my feet fall to the floor. One of the great things about my room is the floor. We always had wall-to-wall carpeting in New York City, but now my room has a wood floor, made out of these old, gnarled-up planks that seem really solid. It's a little cold sometimes, but it makes for great acoustics when I'm playing my drums.

I tiptoed over to the door and pulled it open

to listen for a minute. I could tell from the silence that M was still sleeping. She must have slept right through her own alarm. Even though M is not exactly morning material, either, she's always up before me. Usually she has to scream up the stairs for ten minutes to get me cranking.

Well, today I was going to turn the tables. I shuffled over to my drums and slumped down on the stool. Then I picked up my sticks and tried to give them a little twirl. Not a good idea: My fingers weren't exactly awake yet.

I took a couple of deep breaths and then slammed into a Led Zeppelin drum riff that rattled the windows. At first I was still so sleepy that I missed a couple of beats, but pretty soon I was wide awake and jamming big time.

When I finished, I looked up to see M standing in my doorway wearing her totally unbelievable "stern parent" expression. "Very funny," she growled.

"I knew you wouldn't want to oversleep," I said sweetly.

"I guess a quiet little 'wake up' would have been out of the question?" M asked.

"Totally," I shot back.

M kind of grunted. "Well, you make the tea. I get the shower first." She headed down the stairs and called back up to me, "And I'm not going to leave you any hot water."

Twenty minutes later we were both showered and dressed. M wore a paint-splattered smock over paint-splattered jeans and a pair of paint-splattered loafers. I knew that after she started working at the big canvas in her studio, it was only a question of time before she was paint-splattered, too.

I had on a pair of two-tone leggings that were black on the outside and electric blue on the inner part. Over those I wore a black miniskirt and this great oversized sweatshirt that has a grainy-looking black-and-white picture of John Lennon flashing a peace sign on the back. I'd slipped on my black high-tops, leaving the laces kind of untied.

"Looking sharp," M commented. Then she looked at me sideways over her cup of chamomile tea. "Some reason why you're up early and playing Led Zeppelin?"

I shrugged my shoulders and poured myself a cup of tea. "I just woke up, is all."

"I guess your dad being in town had nothing to do with it, huh?" M smiled. "Peter always did have a talent for making life seem exciting."

I couldn't argue with that. But I had to wonder, if M thought D was so exciting, how she could possibly think Terry the Tame was in D's league. High school history teacher from Acorn Falls versus a totally with-it TV director and producer from New York City? No contest.

"By the way, did D happen to mention that he'd broken up with Leighton?" I asked as I sat down. I tried to sound casual, but it came out kind of blunt, which is me all over. M says I'm about as subtle as a two-ton truck.

M looked at me thoughtfully. She was trying to figure out what I was feeling, but she knew me too well just to ask straight out. Besides, I guess she also knows that I'll tell her on my own — as soon as I figure out for myself what's going on in my brain.

"Yes, Ran," she said at last. "He mentioned that he was no longer with Leighton." She took a sip of her tea and waited to see if I was going to ask another question. I wanted to ask if it made her kind of glad that D was no longer involved with anybody. But M answered my question before I could get around to asking it.

"I'm sorry that your father is going through this unhappiness," she said softly. "I don't like to think he might be lonely."

I could barely stop myself from saying something dumb, like, "Why don't you have dinner with him? Maybe now you two could think about trying again." But I kept my mouth shut. M and D had both always been careful not to drag me into the middle of their problems. And I guess I knew I had to stay out of them now.

"Sabs and Katie were major league impressed by D last night," I said. "He's going to give Al a part in the commercial he's shooting. And Sabs can't stop asking him about all the rockers and Hollywood people he knows. It's like he's her own personal fan magazine."

"That's nice," M said. "And what do your friends say about Terry?"

Like I said, there's no point in trying to be subtle around M. We're too much alike, and she can always read me on the important things. I'd been talking about how great D was, and she'd known that all along I meant "compared to Terry."

"Spike says he's a great history teacher," I admitted. "He claims he actually manages to stay awake in Terry's class."

"But he's not quite in your dad's league, right?"

I winced. M was not about to let me off the hook easily. I looked down at my cup of tea.

"Listen, Ran, your dad is a very special man. And most important, he's your father. So I hope you always believe that your dad is the greatest guy on earth, and that no one else can measure up to him. I know I still feel like that about my father."

M reached across the table and took my hand. "But I also think you need to give Terry a chance. Maybe he's not your father, but that doesn't mean he's not a good guy."

I didn't say anything. What could I say? I just shoved back my chair and pointed at the clock. "Gotta motor," I said quietly. "Big frog-guts quiz in science today."

I grabbed my books and my black bomber jacket and took off before one of us said something we'd be sorry about. No way was I going to sit around and hear about what a swell dude Terry was. He wasn't D. Enough said.

I was still thinking about what M had said when I got to school. But as soon as I arrived, I was jarred out of my funk by the amazing Bradley Junior High Rumor Machine.

The first encounter was with Arizonna. "R.Z.!" he shouted, weaving in and out of the crowd in the hallway. "Babe! Like you never told me your old man was such a major dude. I am wigged. Like your old man and the ultimate beach tune! I told Sabs 'No way,' but she said, 'Way.'"

Sometimes Arizonna can be a little hard to understand. When he gets excited, he slips into complete dudespeak. "Zone, what are you talking about?" I asked.

"Your dad and Brian Wilson, babe."

"Brian Wilson," I repeated blankly.

"Main dude of the Beach Boys," Arizonna said. His tone of voice made it clear that only someone from another planet wouldn't know who Brian Wilson was. "Like your dad wrote the lyrics for 'Surfin' Safari'? That is like the most excellent surfing tune ever."

I rolled my eyes. "Zone, my dad was about five years old when the Beach Boys cut 'Surfin' Safari.'"

"But I heard Nick say that Sam said that Sabs told him —" he began.

Just then some girl I didn't even know came up and grabbed my shoulder. "Your father was Paula Abdul's dancing coach? That is so —"

"Untrue," I interrupted her. "I don't even know if my dad knows how to dance." I shook my head in amazement. Obviously the stories about D were only going to get more extreme — and they were pretty extreme already. School hadn't even started. By the end of the day, D would probably be the fifth Beatle or Madonna's one true love or something.

I spent most of the day shaking my head and going, "No, no, no."

One good thing happened because of all the rumors, though. Katie, Sabs, Al, and I were at lunch when Stacy the Great and her girl gang came marching up to our table.

Stacy gave a flip of her long blond hair. I did my patented "Stacy Flip" right back, just to be polite. I figured it was sort of like a high-five for snobs.

"Rowena," she began in her superior tone, "I just wanted to let you know that my father once went to a banquet with Mrs. Bush. And a First

Lady of the whole United States is better than a bunch of rock stars."

As always, Stacy was bound and determined to be just a little bit better than anyone else. Listening to tales about D all day must have really gotten under her skin. And maybe her story was actually true. It sounded too dumb to be made up.

I heard Katie stifling a laugh. "That's very interesting, Stacy," I said seriously. "I never knew that about your father." I stood up so other tables around us could hear. "Listen, everyone," I said loudly, "Stacy says Mr. Hansen used to date Barbara Bush."

I sat down, and the whole table exploded with laughter. "That's — that's not —" Stacy spluttered. But the more she protested, the more everyone laughed. Finally, with a last poisonous look at me, she spun on her heel and stomped away, trailing her clones.

After school I waited out on the sidewalk for D to arrive. Katie and Sabs went on to Fitzie's, but Al decided to keep me company. I think she understood how stoked I was about spending some one-on-one with D.

I looked up and down the street. No limo.

"He'll probably be a little late," I told Al. "He gets tied up with business sometimes."

But just as the words were out of my mouth, the limo pulled around the corner and cruised to a stop right in front of us. As I reached for the door handle, Paul jumped out of the driver's seat.

"Ms. Zak," he said breathlessly, "I'm afraid your father couldn't make it. He sends his apologies, but business matters have cropped up and —"

"Right," I interrupted. "No need to go into the whole apology thing." I've always figured apologies were unnecessary, although I guess I've had to make one or two myself. "It's cool," I told Paul. "I understand. D's in a tough business."

I turned away quickly. I wasn't exactly feeling real great, but I didn't want to make a big scene in front of Paul. I mean, he was just some dude doing his job. I wasn't going to lay my problems on him.

"It must be complicated trying to handle all of his business from here in Minnesota," Al said gently.

"Sure." I nodded. "Things get out of control

when you're away from the office." I knew Al was trying to make me feel better, but it was just making me feel worse to have her feeling sorry for me. I really hate that.

"Mr. Zak did say that you girls should be ready bright and early tomorrow morning to go on the commercial shoot," Paul added. "And . . . are you Ms. Cloud?" he asked Al.

"Yes. I'm Allison Cloud."

"Good." Paul leaned into the limo and retrieved a manila envelope. "These are permission forms you need to have your parents sign," he said, handing the envelope to Al. "Work permission, model release, and so on."

Al took the envelope. Paul tipped his hat in that professional way chauffeurs are supposed to. Then he climbed into the car and drove off.

Al stood there, fingering the envelope.

"I guess you don't feel like going to Fitzie's," she said quietly.

"No," I answered just as quietly.

She knew I wasn't in the mood to hang with the crowd at Fitzie's. But she'd asked me so it wouldn't look like such a big deal that D had just stiffed me.

After a few moments Al asked, "Want to

come to my house for a while?"

At that instant I couldn't say anything at all. I just bent down and retied my shoelaces. I couldn't believe that my eyes were starting to sting with tears. On top of everything else, now I was really mad at my father for making me mad.

Finally I stood up and said, "No, I think I'll do a little practicing on my drums."

"Ran," Al said, "I'm sure it would have to be very important business before your dad would cancel out on you like this."

Usually Al knows just the right thing to say to make me feel better. But this time she couldn't help. Because all I was thinking was that somehow, no matter how busy he was, D had managed to remember about Al.

Chapter Six

On Saturday morning I rolled out of bed a little slower than I had the day before. Not that I was expecting the worst, or anything. And even though it was the day of the commercial shoot, I just wasn't quite as excited as I had been before.

When I got home yesterday, I think M guessed pretty quickly what had happened. It wasn't like D hadn't ever stood one of us up before. I'd heard plenty of excuses from D, back when we were all still living together in New York City. And she'd heard plenty herself.

I guess M figured that I was just going to have to deal with everything my own way. Which was cool by me, because I don't think talking about problems makes them better. I'm just not into the whole Oprah kind of thing. You know what I mean: Let's all sit around and whine and then hug each other a lot.

I was still sipping my tea that morning when I heard someone blowing a car horn out front. M went over to the window and checked it out. "It's your limo," she said cheerfully.

"Right," I said, getting up. "I'll catch you later, M."

Paul had already picked up Katie and Al and Sabs. When I climbed into the limo, Sabs was cross-examining D, hoping to dig up more good celebrity gossip.

"I thought I'd better get you last, honey," D said. "I know how you like to sleep in on Saturdays." He gave me a wink. "And on Sundays and Mondays and Tuesdays. . . ."

I tried not to smile, but I couldn't help it. Then D leaned over toward me and slipped a small package out of his pocket.

"It's fresh from the factory," he whispered. "Not even released to the distributors yet, and it won't be in the stores for another month."

I picked up the package and tore off the wrapping. Inside was Broken Arrow's latest CD — the one everybody in the whole country was dying to get their hands on.

"When I realized I was going to have to break our date to go shopping for tunes," D explained, "I had this air-expressed." He looked right at me, waiting until I made eye contact. "I'm sorry about yesterday, Ran. Really sorry."

I looked down at the CD and grinned. It was impossible to stay mad at D for long. What could I say? If I copped some major attitude about the whole deal, it would have just turned the whole day into a downer. Besides, he really had gone to a lot of trouble to make things up to me.

"So, Paul," I said loudly. "You got a CD player back here somewhere?"

"Sure do," Paul said.

"Then we're going to have the world premiere of the newest from Broken Arrow." I stuck the CD in the player slot and hit PLAY. Then in my D.J. voice I yelled, "All right, then, let's get pumped!" and cranked up the volume till the wheels vibrated.

The CD had just about ended when I looked out the window and realized we were pulling into a small airport that's fairly close to Acorn Falls.

"What's with the airport?" I asked D.

D grinned. "It's a surprise! The shoot is too far north, so we're going to fly."

"We're going on a plane!" Sabs squealed. "Isn't it incredible?"

"But how did you organize this?" I asked, looking from D to Sabs to Al and Katie.

Allison giggled. "Peter called all of our parents and got their permission to let us fly. Isn't this totally cool!"

I couldn't believe that my father had gone to all this trouble for my friends — for me! I was absolutely speechless!

Soon we turned off the highway onto an exit for the airport. The limo came to a stop in front of a small jet with two engines near the tail.

"It looks a little smaller than the plane I flew on when I went to see my aunt in New Mexico," Katie commented doubtfully. "Are you sure that thing is safe?"

D shrugged. "It got me here from New York. It's a charter jet that I use sometimes."

"Like to visit rock stars?" Sabs said. Sabs was not giving up easily on the celebrity thing.

"Sure," D said to Sabs. "Or to take future movie stars like you on short trips."

We climbed on board and buckled ourselves into these fairly plush seats. A few minutes later the jet took off. Taking off in a plane is a major rush. It's the same feeling I get when I'm skateboarding and I go airborne, only about a thousand times more intense.

We were only in the air for about an hour before we could feel the jet starting to descend. The ground below us was completely white with snow, except for a few little roads that looked like dark pieces of string. Up ahead you could see blinding sunlight being reflected off a small lake.

I think Katie was a little nervous about the landing. I guess she's not real big on flying, like a lot of people. I saw her clenching the arms of her seat and closing her eyes, but Katie, being Katie, was too brave to make a federal case out of it.

As we all ran down the steps, I realized what a small airport it was. Just a short runway and a hangar, really, with a few beat-up-looking old planes parked nearby. A big four-wheel-drive Jeep was waiting for us. There was a young bearded dude wearing a red parka behind the wheel.

"The location's all set up, Mr. Z.," the driver told D. "We got that generator problem whipped an hour ago."

"Let's get going, then," D said, suddenly all business. "I don't want to lose the light."

The five of us piled into the back of the Jeep. About a mile from the airport, it suddenly veered off the road, tearing right across a snow-covered field and into the trees.

The driver was definitely into the off-road experience, and I had to hang on to the door handle to keep from being bounced around like a pinball. Suddenly the driver slammed on the brakes and skidded to a stop, sending snow flying everywhere.

We sat there for a minute, just trying to catch our breath. Personally, I was feeling relieved I was still alive and in one piece. Sabs was looking a little green. Katie didn't look too hot herself. "All right," she announced, rubbing her rear end, "I am officially no longer afraid of flying. Now I'm afraid of Jeeps."

We climbed out slowly and took a look around. I had been "on location" with D before, so I pretty much knew what to expect. People were dashing around crazily, but D seemed perfectly calm. There were makeup people, and wardrobe, and cameras, but the thing you notice first is the lighting. Even when you're filming outside in bright sunlight, there are lots of extra lights on poles, along with big mirrors that focus the sunlight.

Sabs took a long look at all the snow and the beautiful blue lake. "It's so . . . so . . . Hollywood," she said in an amazed voice, which was funny because it was all really very Minnesota, if you know what I mean. But I think she was imagining herself someday, acting in front of the cameras.

Al seemed less enthusiastic. I kind of got the feeling from the look on her face that she just wanted to get the whole thing over with. "Um, Mr. Zak?" she asked D nervously. "Where should I go?"

"Consuelo!" D shouted. A chubby young woman came running, stomping through the snow in a pair of obviously brand-new L. L. Bean boots. She did not look like she was happy to be in the middle of Nowhere, Minnesota.

"Wonderful location, Mr. Z," she said sarcastically. "All my makeup supplies are half-frozen."

"Consuelo, meet Allison Cloud." He pointed at Al. "She's doing the lead. I want her ready to go — makeup, wardrobe — in fifteen minutes."

"But —" Consuelo began.

"No buts," D broke in. "Fifteen."

Consuelo rolled her eyes. Then she grabbed Al by the arm and marched her away like she was under arrest.

"Anything we can do, D?" I asked. "Or should we just stay out of the way?" I'd been around sets enough to know that things can get pretty frantic.

"That's fine, hon," D said in a distracted voice. Then he turned back to look at Katie and Sabs and me. He had this curious kind of look on his face, like an idea had just occurred to him. "Any of you girls know how to throw a ball well?"

Sabs and I immediately looked at Katie. Katie was the only certified jock in our group. "I guess so," Katie said doubtfully.

"Good. Practice throwing snowballs at that tree over there. I'll call you when I need you."

"Why —" Katie began, but D was already long gone.

"What was that all about?" Katie asked me.

"I'm clueless," I admitted. "But he wouldn't have asked you if it wasn't important."

"All right," Katie said. "You guys going to come with me?"

"Sure," I said. "Nothing's going to happen for at least fifteen minutes, till Al's ready."

We headed off to a nearby grove of trees and watched Katie warm up. She started off pretty weak, but after a while she was hitting her tree almost every time. Sabs and I both tried a little target practice, too, but, like I said, Katie's the only jock.

Suddenly we noticed the kamikaze Jeep driver dashing toward us. "Snowball thrower on the set!" he shouted.

Sabs and Katie and I all took off after him. When we got back to the set, we saw Al, looking kind of orange in her heavy makeup. Her jeans were so tight, she could barely move. I have to say, she did not look especially happy. D was walking beside her, showing her exactly where to step and when to turn her head toward the camera.

They went over it again and again. Al was supposed to come running out from behind a fake bush, take four really big steps, turn, look at the camera, flash a major smile, then fall facedown in the snow and come up laughing. Then she had to say, in her most mellow voice, "Cubex Jeans — more than cool."

D was being very patient, explaining everything to Al very carefully and kidding with her a little to get her to relax. He was completely focused on her, but then, he had to be, I reminded myself. This was his work, and Al was a part of it.

D stood back, arms crossed over his chest, and watched as Al practiced the routine. After a couple of tries, he told her to take bigger, exaggerated steps. Everything in a commercial is overdone that way, sort of bigger than life. You can't just be happy in a commercial — you have to look HAPPY!!!

"Beautiful, Allison," D called out as Al bounded along through the snow. "Perfect. Okay, now the fall." Al dropped into the snow, which was soft enough to cushion her, and came up halfway smiling as she tried to wipe some snow out of her left eye.

"Hmmm," D said, his eyes narrowed. "That's going to be the tough part. But not to worry. Take five, Allison. Then we go for real."

Allison came over to join us. She looked a little dazed. "We haven't even started and I'm already cold and worn out," she complained. "Plus these jeans are so tight, it's ridiculous, and my face is stiff from all this makeup."

"It's the price of being a star." Sabs sniffed. "Real professionals would never complain about small inconveniences like that."

"I never claimed I was a real professional," Al pointed out. "What have you guys been doing, anyway?"

"Throwing snowballs," Katie answered. "At trees. Mr. Zak told me to." She shrugged her shoulders. "Don't even bother asking me why, Al, because I don't know."

"Snowballs!" a voice shouted.

"Do they mean me?" Katie wondered aloud.

"Snowball girl, over here!" D's assistant screamed.

"I think they want you now," I told Katie. "The guy in the blue down jacket over there."

"I'm going, too," Sabs declared. "I want to find out what all this snowball tossing is for. Good luck, Al."

Sabs and Katie trudged off, leaving Al and

me alone. Once again I felt a twinge of jealousy toward Al. She'd spent more one-on-one time with D so far than I had, and I guess I was feeling kind of left out.

"You okay, Randy?" Al asked softly.

"I'm cool," I said. It wasn't exactly a lie. I wanted to be cool, and I was trying to be. But I couldn't help thinking that my whole life I'd always had to compete with D's work, and now my best friend was part of that work. It didn't seem fair.

Al sighed. "This is really kind of tough. I was thinking about telling your dad I don't want to do it anymore."

"Are you crazy?" I said. "He's ready to film. You can't walk out now."

"I can if it's what you want me to do," Al said, meeting my eyes.

I looked away and kicked at a clump of snow with my boot. Al was such a good friend, she was willing to give up the money from the commercial if it would make me happy.

"Allison! We're ready!" D shouted. "Let's do this thing, people."

I looked at Al and gave her a big grin. "Go

ahead, Al," I said. "Knock 'em dead."

"If you say so," she said a little doubtfully.

Al took her place, and I moved forward to a spot where I could take in all the action. I saw Katie and Sabs hunched down beneath camera one. There was a small pyramid of snowballs nearby.

"Action!" D yelled.

Al ran out from behind the fake bush, taking big, high steps. She turned toward the camera, then ran forward and dived facedown into the snow. Just like she was supposed to, she came up smiling. But while she was flashing her very best grin, Katie let fly with a snowball that caught Al right in the face.

"Katie!" I yelled. "What are you doing?"

"Your dad told me to," she said helplessly.

"Not bad," D said. "Not bad at all, Allison. Only, next time, I want you to look like getting hit in the face with a snowball is the most fun you've ever had. Then say your line."

"I'm sorry, Mr. Zak," Al said apologetically, "but I had snow up my nose."

"Welcome to show biz," D said, laughing. He gave Katie a thumbs-up sign. "Good shot, only aim for the bridge of her nose."

"Will do," Katie said.

I ran over and hunched down beside Sabs and Katie, careful to stay below the camera lens. We watched as Al marched gamely back behind her bush.

"Take two," D announced. "And action!"

Out came Al, high-stepping and happy. She turned, came toward the camera, and dived into the snow. This time Katie's snowball caught Al right in the mouth. Before she could manage a smile, she had to spit out a mouthful of snow.

Sabs was the first one to start giggling.

"Shh," Katie whispered. "I need to concentrate."

But of course by that time I was snickering, too. Katie took one look at me and started laughing hysterically. Something about dignified, beautiful Allison spitting out snow while she tried to grin and say her line was just plain funny. Al pretended to be mad, but we could all tell she was having a great time.

Consuelo came out and fixed Al's makeup, and another guy rushed over with a portable hair dryer and dried her hair. Meanwhile, our bearded driver spread shovelfuls of fresh snow for Al to fall in. Then they started the whole process all over again.

Take three. Katie missed and the snowball flew past Al's head.

Take four. Al tripped while she was bounding through the snow.

Take five. The snowball stuck to Al's bangs. It looked like she had some huge monster zit growing out of her forehead.

By take six Sabs, Katie, and I were in pain from laughing so much.

By take nine I had totally forgotten that I had ever been jealous of Al.

On the way home in the plane and the limo, all Allison managed to say was "Twenty-eight takes" in this kind of amazed voice. "Twenty-eight takes."

When we dropped her off at her house that afternoon, I said, "Catch you tomorrow, Al."

She just gazed at me with a glassy stare. "Twenty-eight takes, Randy," she muttered. "Twenty-eight."

As we drove on to the barn, D told me he hoped I would check on Al to make sure she was all right. "I think she had kind of a rough day," he remarked. "I hope it wasn't too tough on her, but we only had the one day and we had to get it right."

"I'm sure she'll be fine as soon as her face thaws out," I joked.

"Listen, Ran," D said, "if you're willing to take another chance on me, there's something tonight that I'd like to take you to."

"Not another commercial, I hope."

"No, kind of a party. Broken Arrow is having a little get-together tonight in Minneapolis. It's a release party for the video that goes with the new album. Since I directed it, I'm invited. Me and a guest."

I was just slightly excited. In fact I screamed so loud I think Paul nearly drove the limo into a tree. "A party with Broken Arrow? They're actually going to be there? I mean, like, for real? Them? And me?"

"That's the general idea," D said, laughing. "So I guess we're on?"

I jumped out as the limo came to a stop. "Just try and stop me," I said with an ear-to-ear grin. "We are most definitely on, D. Most definitely."

Chapter Seven

"Randy, you look awesome!" M exclaimed.

"Acorn Falls awesome, or New York City awesome?" I asked as I struck a pose in the kitchen early that evening.

"New York – London – Paris awesome," M assured me.

As soon as I'd gotten home from the shoot that afternoon, I'd gone into high gear, trying to find just the right look for the party. I'd been working on it for hours. Usually I'm pretty sure of myself when it comes to clothes. I mean, I have my own look, and it's definitely not the preppie pastel style everybody at Bradley goes for. But it had been a while since I'd been around someone who knew what was really hot. Not since my friend Sheck had come to visit, in fact. Who knew? Maybe I'd fallen behind the ol' fashion curve. After all, in Acorn Falls, people thought wearing a black turtleneck was a major fashion risk.

I'd finally decided on my black suede minidress. It has a big suede jacket covered with silver studs in this kind of abstract design. I borrowed these big silver hoops of M's and added a couple of smaller black hoops for my right ear.

I'm not exactly sure why it mattered so much to me what I wore to the opening. I guess I just wanted everything to be perfect. Ever since he'd gotten to Acorn Falls, I'd sort of been feeling like D and I weren't exactly on the same wavelength. He was still in his New York frame of mind, buzzing around at warp speed.

The more I thought about it, the more I realized that that was probably why he'd forgotten about taking me shopping the day before. And why he hadn't paid a whole lot of attention to me during the shoot. He had a lot more on his mind than I did. It was only natural that he had to focus more on other things. Business was business, after all.

M finished rinsing out the last of her brushes in the sink. That's one problem with her studio. It doesn't have a separate sink. She can really trash the one in the kitchen when she's in one of her creative periods. During her papier-mâché phase she was really dangerous, stopping up the sink practically every day. The Roto-Rooter guy really became a close personal friend of ours.

"What time is D picking you up?" M asked.

"He said sevenish," I answered. "So any minute now."

"You want something to eat before you go?"

I shook my head. "There'll be plenty of munchies at the party."

M yanked open the fridge door. It was a pretty sad sight. A lump of tofu. Half a carton of kefir, this yogurt drink she loves. And some of that yak cheese or whatever it was, with a very interesting crop of mold growing on it.

"How's that penicillin experiment coming along?" I joked. I peered over her shoulder. "Sorry. I meant to go by the store yesterday and pick up some stuff."

When M gets caught up in an art project, I sort of pick up the slack on the housework front. I like it that way. We have it down to a system, the two of us. Well, *usually* we do, anyway. Every system has its glitches.

"It's my fault," M said. "I've been so preoccupied with this painting the past few days."

That's not all you've been preoccupied with, I thought to myself, but I didn't say anything. I knew if I brought up Terry, M would just start giving me her "He's a great guy" routine, and I really wasn't up for an encore performance.

"How's the painting coming, anyway?" I asked. She was working on this huge canvas, so big it practically filled one whole wall of her studio. It was the first time she'd worked on such a large scale.

"Not bad," she said, closing the fridge door with a sigh. "But the canvas is buckling a bit because it's so big. I need to tighten it up somehow."

"What did D say when he saw it?" I asked. He'd taken a quick tour of the barn the day he'd picked me up at Fitzie's, but he hadn't stayed long. Pretty much his only comment had been "This reminds me of an episode of 'Green Acres,' Liv." That's this old TV series where some rich New Yorkers go live in the boondocks on a farm. They rerun it late at night sometimes.

M had just laughed when D said that. "Once a hick, always a hick," she'd said. I guess she was talking about the fact that she was born here in Acorn Falls, but I got the feeling there was more to it than that.

"Peter didn't say much about my work," M said. "You know your dad. He doesn't always give compliments very well."

"I just wish D understood how important your art is to you," I said.

"He does, in his own way," M said thoughtfully. "Besides, what matters is that I think it's important."

I reached over and gave her a quick hug. "I'm really proud of you, you know?"

"Ditto," M said, grinning. She headed off to shower (she was covered with paint, as usual). I checked the clock on the stove. Seven-thirty. Still in the "sevenish" range, as far as D was concerned. When it came to being on time, he definitely had his own idea of things.

I sat there thinking about what M had said about her painting. Maybe I'd been insane to think she and D could ever get back together. They were awfully different. More different than ever, now. I hadn't really thought about how much M had changed since coming to Acorn Falls. Come to think of it, I guess I'd probably changed some, too.

A few minutes later there was a knock at the door. Finally! I checked my reflection in the mirror in the living room and dashed for the door. "Let's jam!" I cried as I swung it open.

I felt like a jerk as soon as the words were out of my mouth. It wasn't D who was standing there. It was Terry.

My face must have said it all, because Terry asked, "Why do I get the feeling I'm a letdown?"

"Sorry." I held open the door and he stepped inside. He was carrying a brown paper bag in one hand. "My dad's coming over any minute," I said kind of abruptly, by way of explanation. I was hoping he'd take the hint, but he just stood there.

"Ran, is that Peter?" my mom called as she stepped out of the bathroom. She'd changed into her jeans and a sweatshirt and was toweling her hair. "Oh, Terry," she said, looking over in surprise. I think she may have even blushed a little — definitely not your usual M reaction.

"Sorry to barge in like this, Olivia —" Terry began.

"Don't be silly," M said quickly. She tossed

her towel on the couch and combed her fingers through her hair. "Have you eaten? I was just going to phone Ho Lin's for some kung pao chicken and lo mein."

Terry narrowed his eyes. "What? No crispy prawns and walnuts?"

M laughed. "I see you've made the acquaintance of Ho Lin's."

"Are you kidding? I keep them in business."

M headed for the phone. "So you'll stay?"

Terry sent a quick glance in my direction. "You sure you two didn't have other plans?"

"Go ahead." I gave a casual wave. "I've got a better offer."

"Randy's dad is taking her to a party in Minneapolis," M explained. "It's for the debut of a new music video he produced."

"Broken Arrow," I added. Not that Terry would know who they were. He seemed like the kind of guy whose musical taste ran more toward Zamfir and his pan flute.

"Never heard of them, I'm afraid." Terry shook his head apologetically. His glasses started a slow dive off his nose, and he pushed them back into place with his finger. "I'm sorry to confess I've never actually sat through an entire video on MTV. My kids at school tell me I'm a real musical dinosaur."

It figured. "You don't know what you're missing. Music videos are the newest art form," I said, quoting something I'd heard D say once. I glanced out the window, tapping my foot impatiently. Where was D, anyway? The party was supposed to start at eight, and Minneapolis was a good hour's drive.

"Speaking of art," Terry said, reaching into the paper bag he was carrying, "that's why I stopped by, Olivia. I was over at Carson's Hardware this afternoon to pick up some stuff, and I noticed they had this pair of heavy-duty pliers. You mentioned you were having trouble with your canvas, and I thought maybe I could give you a hand tightening it up."

"That was awfully thoughtful of you, Terry," M said, looking really pleased.

"This way, when you've got a show at a famous museum someday, I can say I had a small part in your success," Terry said.

I smiled in spite of myself. It was nice to see M had another fan, even if it was Terry.

M picked up the phone and dialed Ho Lin's. We call them so much, we have the number on auto dial, right after the fire department. "Ran," she asked, "why don't I order you something? You're going to be starving by the time you get to the party."

"I'd rather wait," I muttered. My stomach was growling so loud, you could have heard it in the next county, but I wanted to wait for D.

So I waited. And waited. And waited. Terry helped M fix her canvas, and by then the food had shown up. They begged me to join them, but I just sat on the love seat in the living room, drumming my fingers on the windowsill. I absolutely hate waiting around for people. But it wasn't like I had a whole lot of choice.

Terry sat there with M, going on and on about how great her paintings were, but I was only half listening.

Mostly I was wondering if D was actually going to leave me stranded there all night, looking like a complete and total idiot. I don't think I've ever been so mad at D, not ever. Once was bad enough. But twice? I mean, I'm as understanding as the next person, but this was way out of line. (Okay, so maybe I'm not the most understanding person on the planet. That still didn't excuse what D was doing.)

"So, Randy, Olivia tells me you're into Buddy Rich," Terry said as he and M began to clean up after dinner.

"Yeah," I said sullenly. When I'm mad, I absolutely hate to talk to anybody. What I really felt like doing was hopping on my skateboard and cruising. But the roads were pretty slick, and besides, I was still hanging on to this stupid fantasy that D was going to show up at the last minute. I knew it was stupid, but I just couldn't stop hoping. I think that's what burned me more than anything.

"I've got a recording on CD of his last live concert that'll blow your mind," Terry called from the kitchen.

· Reluctantly I pulled myself away from the window. "I didn't think that was on CD yet."

Terry nodded. "It was just released. I special-ordered it."

I frowned. "I thought you weren't into music."

"Depends on the music," Terry said with a grin. "I'm just discriminating."

Well, that was one small point in Terry's favor. I figured if he was a fan of my all-time favorite drummer, he couldn't be all bad.

"You know, I've got that CD out in the junkmobile, if you want to borrow it," Terry offered.

"You've got a CD player in that thing?"

"Who's gonna rip it off?" Terry asked. "That's the last car on earth anyone would expect to find a decent sound system in. Most people are surprised to find a motor in it." He hooked a thumb toward the door. "Come on. I'll prove to you I'm not a total musical ignoramus."

I cast M a "what the heck" glance and pulled on my quilted coat. Then I followed Terry out to his old Dart. It was dark, and the interior lights didn't work, so I had to hold this flashlight he kept in the front seat while he dug around for his CD holder. There was about a three-foot pile of fast-food trash in the backseat.

"Does M know you eat at Burger King?" I asked as he tossed a milk shake cup into the front seat.

"I think she's hoping to reform me," he replied. "But I won't give up my Whoppers for any woman." He glanced over his shoulder and winked. "Even Olivia."

I laughed in spite of myself. "Your secret's

safe with me. I still get cravings for a Big Mac sometimes, but M says it's all a matter of willpower."

At last Terry emerged from the backseat with his cassette holder. "I'm convinced if I work on her long enough, your mom'll repent and realize that a wad of tofu just can't compete with a nice greasy fry."

Okay, so that was another small point in Terry's favor.

Back in the house, I checked out his CDs. He had this amazing collection of Buddy Rich's stuff, not to mention some older jazz stuff I wasn't really familiar with. I couldn't believe he kept all these great tunes in that old heap. I picked out a few and he recommended some more, and we cranked up the CD player. For a while I just sat back and closed my eyes and listened. But pretty soon I felt like cutting loose, so I grabbed my sticks and jammed along on the coffee table.

M brewed up a pot of ginseng tea and microwaved some of the leftover lo mein for me. Then, after I ate, we just sat there together, getting into the tunes. It was nice, really, and for a while I even forgot about D standing me up.

But then I glanced at the clock and thought about how I should have been at the party right then, and all my anger at D came back again and hit me like a slap in the face.

It was weird. Normally I would have hopped on my board or locked myself in my room and slammed out my feelings on my drums. As I said, when I'm mad about something, I am not exactly what you'd call good company. I'm sure Terry and M knew how upset I was, but they didn't say anything, which was a very smart move on their part.

I guess it was because they left me alone that I stuck around and kept jamming with Buddy Rich. It wasn't so bad, really, the three of us sitting there together, all caught up in the beat. The music was so good, I could almost manage to forget everything else.

Almost.

Chapter Eight

D calls Randy.

RANDY: Speak to me.

D: Ran? It's D.

RANDY: Oh. (*Pauses*) Hi, D.
What's happening?

D: Ran, honey, I can't begin to tell you how sorry I am.

RANDY: About what?

D: About standing you up last night. It's just that —

RANDY: Hey, it's cool. No biggie.

D: Ran, I know how excited you were, and —

RANDY: D, I said it was cool. You don't think I really expected to go to that party with you, do you? I mean, I understand how business is. You got tied up, or whatever. Like I said, cool by me.

D: (*Sighs.*) Ran, will it do any good if
            I promise you I will never, ever let
            something like this happen again?

Randy doesn't answer.

D: Hon, you still there?

RANDY: Yeah. Listen, I have to go. Busy
            day. Lots of plans.

D: Ran, don't hang up.

Randy: Gotta go. Later.

Randy hangs up.
A minute later she calls Allison.

MRS.
CLOUD: Cloud residence.

RANDY: Hi, Mrs. Cloud, it's Randy Zak.
            How's the baby?

MRS.
CLOUD: She's doing fine — she smiles all
            the time. Hang on a minute. I'll
            get Allison.

ALLISON: Hey, Randy. How was the party
            last night?

RANDY: Well, that kind of didn't work out.

ALLISON: That's too bad.

RANDY: No biggie. Stuff happens, you
            know? But I think maybe I'll do

some skateboarding today. I'm not really psyched for the mall.

ALLISON: No problem. We can do it some other time.

RANDY: I'm just up for some serious thrashing, you know? I haven't ridden my board in days.

ALLISON: I understand. Call me later?

RANDY: You know it. *Ciao.*

Allison calls Katie.

KATIE: Campbell and Beauvais residence, Katherine speaking.

ALLISON: Katie? Al. I just got off the phone with Randy.

KATIE: Hey, how was the big party?

ALLISON: She didn't exactly say so, but I think her dad pulled another no-show.

KATIE: You're kidding! Again?

ALLISON: I'm afraid Randy's really upset. She's blowing off the mall today.

KATIE: I don't blame her. What's she doing, playing her drums or skateboarding?

ALLISON: Skateboarding. Katie, she sounded so sad. Not that she really said anything. You know Randy.

KATIE: What is the problem with her dad? He seems so cool, and then he just keeps pulling things like this. That really burns me. I don't care how busy he is.

ALLISON: I know, and she always makes excuses for him.

KATIE: I wish there was something we could do.

ALLISON: Her dad is leaving tomorrow.

KATIE: That's probably good.

ALLISON: Maybe, but Randy will be depressed. And I think we should be there for her, even though she probably won't want anybody around.

KATIE: You can count on me. Randy's house before school?

ALLISON: Right. I'll call Sabs.

Allison calls Sabs.
Sabs and Sam pick up the phone extensions at exactly the same time.

SABS: Hello.

SAM: Hello, too.

ALLISON: It's me, Allison.

SABS: It's for me, Sam.

SAM: Not necessarily. Maybe Allison has called me for some intelligent conversation. Did you ever think of that possibility?

ALLISON
AND SABS: (*Together*) No!

SAM: Fine. I know when I've been insulted.

Sam hangs up.

SABS: Okay, he's gone.

ALLISON: Hi, Sabs. I'm calling about Ran.

SABS: (*Groans.*) Oh, don't tell me. Something went wrong with the party, right?

ALLISON: How did you know?

SABS: I didn't, but your voice sounded sad, and besides, I kind of figured something would go wrong. After all, her dad isn't exactly the most reliable guy on earth.

ALLISON: Well, Randy didn't really tell me much. You know how she gets when she's bummed. She just called to say she doesn't want to go to the mall with us today.

SABS: Now I don't exactly feel like shopping, either.

ALLISON: I know what you mean. Listen, Sabs. Do you think Randy was mad that I ended up spending so much time with her dad because of the commercial? I kind of feel like I came between them somehow.

SABS: I don't think so. Well, maybe a little. But it wasn't your fault, Al. He offered you a job, after all. Besides, you had to spend the whole day getting hit in the face with snowballs. It wasn't like you were having a good time.

ALLISON: Still . . .

SABS: Al, this is a problem between Randy and her dad. They have to solve it themselves.

ALLISON: He's leaving tomorrow morning.

SABS: Poor Randy. We need to try to do something to cheer her up.

ALLISON: Randy's pretty hard to cheer up when she doesn't want to be cheerful. But I do think we should all kind of drop by her house tomorrow morning before school. You know, to remind her that she's always got us.

SABS: That's a good idea, Al. But I sure hope Randy can make up with her dad. They're such a perfect father-daughter team, if you know what I mean. They're both so . . . you know, interesting.

ALLISON: Hope for the best. I'll see you there.

SABS: Bye.

Chapter Nine

"On your left!" I yelled as I flew past two little kids on the sidewalk. I was going top speed for level ground, but I wanted to go a lot faster. There'd been a little snow the night before, but most of it had melted off the streets already. I gave a hard kick and did a two-wheel turn onto Davis Road.

Crouching lower on my board, I spread my arms out to help me balance. Davis is a pretty steep hill, and soon I was flying like an Olympic skier.

It's scary sometimes, going really all-out fast, but it's also cool because you're so worried about doing a crash and burn that you don't have time to think about anything else. And not thinking seemed like a good idea.

I hit the turn at the bottom of the street, and dropped so low on the board that I was practically sitting down. I almost lost it on the curve, but I pulled it out at the last minute.

I headed for the park. There's a new skateboard ramp there where you can try out new moves. And since, for some reason, there were no other skateboarders around, I had the ramp all to myself.

I thrashed for almost two hours, till the snow started falling. Snow and skateboards don't exactly mix, by the way. Besides, I was getting tired.

It was falling pretty thick as I headed home, coming down in big, fat flakes that could have passed for cotton balls, they were so huge. Unfortunately, snow makes everything seem really quiet. And quiet was not really what I was after.

I figured I'd hit the drums when I got home. I just hoped M wasn't lying in wait, hoping to have a heart-to-heart with me. Even after two hours of serious skateboarding, I was still feeling mad at the world. Or, to be more specific, mad at D.

D had only been in town for a couple of days, and he'd managed to dump me twice. It wasn't so much that I'd just been psyched about going to a party for Broken Arrow. I was psyched, don't get me wrong. But mostly I was excited because it was finally going to be a night with just me and D.

I'd figured we could have talked in the limo on the way to the party. I don't know what about. Whatever, you know? Without Katie and Sabs. And Al.

I kicked hard twice, sending me and my board around the corner onto my street. I halfway expected to see D's limo parked out in front of the barn, but the street was empty. M's car was gone, too.

No heart-to-heart with M. Good. I still needed to chill on my own for a while.

No D, either. No lame apologies and no lame promises. I was relieved. But I guess I was a little disappointed, too. What a sucker. How many more times was he going to have to stand me up before I caught on?

I hopped off my board and flipped it up into my hand. The front door was unlocked. M's always forgetting to lock up. Fortunately, there isn't much crime in Acorn Falls, unlike New York City. In New York, if you leave your front door unlocked, you'll come home and find everything gone but the paint on the walls.

I went straight upstairs. Some serious drumming was what I needed. I mean, I was going to blow the roof off.

As soon as I got upstairs to my room, I felt something different. You know how that is? When you don't know right away exactly what is wrong, but you know it's something?

My room was still a mess — as usual. So it wasn't that. Then, all of a sudden, I saw it. My drums were gone!

But in their place was a new set. An amazing set — totally professional quality. Not that my set was some kid's set, or anything, but you could tell right away that these were dead-serious drums.

Then I heard a movement in the corner of the room behind me. I turned and saw D standing there in the shadows.

"Hi, Ran," he said softly.

"What's happening, D?" I meant to sound very casual, but it didn't even come out sounding like my voice.

"I've been waiting for you," D said. "I sent Paul away with the limo. I even unplugged your phones. No one can reach me. No one can interrupt us."

"D, you don't have to —" I started to say.

"Yes, I do," he said firmly. "I have to. Not just for you, Ran. For me, too." He came closer and looked me straight in the eye. His own eyes were shiny with tears. In my whole life I don't think I've ever seen D cry. I didn't even know it was possible.

"One of the reasons I lost your mother was because I thought work was more important than she was," D said thickly. He cleared his throat. "I refuse to lose you."

"D, you could never —" I had to gulp because for some stupid reason my throat was all tight. Probably from the cold air outside. "You could never lose me," I finished.

D laughed very softly. "You may have noticed that I'm not the greatest father on earth."

I started to say something, but he held up his hand. "No, don't feed me some line, Ran. We both know this fatherhood thing isn't exactly me. I'm not one of those normal, small-town dads who chaperons the school dances and hangs out at PTA meetings."

I couldn't disagree with that. "No, you're not your basic small-town material." D looked down at the ground. "But, D, I'm not exactly small-town material, either."

He looked up at me then and smiled. D has a great smile. He glanced at my leather biker jacket with the two rows of silver studs, and at my spiked hairdo. And then he reached over and put his arms around me, and held me really tight. "No, honey," he agreed. "I guess you're not."

Suddenly he started laughing. And I started laughing, too, even though at the same time my eyes were getting wet, just like his.

"You're the perfect dad for me," I said. I knew it sounded totally corny, but I didn't care. "Only —"

"Only what?" he asked.

"Well, maybe if we had a little more time together sometimes . . ."

He held me even tighter then, and I felt like such a dweeb, because I was crying all over the shoulder of his suit. And I never, ever cry, which made it even worse.

After a long time he let me go. "Hey, you didn't say if you liked the drums. Dune Sadler happened to mention that he was getting a new set, and then I happened to mention that I knew someone who might be able —"

"Those are . . . ?" I wanted to keep going, but my brain had gone into the "closed for lunch" mode. Dune Sadler was the drummer for Broken Arrow. These were Dune's actual very own drums? The drums he had used when he played that incredible solo on "Lizard Talks"?

I gave it another try. "Those are . . . ?"

D nodded. "Dune's old set. I hope you don't mind that they're used."

"Used? Used?" I cried. "Nothing Dune Sadler ever played on is 'used.' More like — like, blessed, or something." I walked toward the drums, almost afraid to touch them.

"He said maybe if you sent him a tape, he could give you a few pointers," D added very nonchalantly. As though getting advice straight from one of the greatest drummers on earth was no big deal.

"Also, he asked me something," D said. "He asked me if you were any good. And I had to admit that I had never really heard you play, not in a very long time. That's when I realized that things would have to change." D took a deep breath. Neither one of us wanted to get all blubbery again. "So, Randy Zak. Are you any good?"

I walked up to the drums and picked up Dune's own sticks. "I could play for you," I said quietly, "you know, if you have just a few minutes to listen." I looked away, prepping myself for the excuse that was about to come. What would it be this time? I wondered vaguely. A call to make? A plane to catch?

"No, Ran. I don't have just a few minutes," D replied. "I have all the time in the world."

I climbed up on my stool and gave the sticks a little twirl. Then I played for about an hour straight. I played better than I ever have in my life, even though it was just for an audience of one.

Later that afternoon M came home, just as D was getting ready to leave. She had a couple of bags of groceries, but I don't believe she'd been shopping for food the whole time. I think she'd deliberately planned to stay away so D and I could have some time alone.

I watched from the stairs as D kissed M on the cheek. Just a friendly kiss, nothing more. They talked for a while, and then D left.

I came down the stairs, kind of making noise

so it wouldn't seem like I had been spying on them. "M!" I yelled. "What's going on?"

"Hi, Ran. What have you and your dad been up to all day?"

I shrugged, giving her my most casual look. "Nothing much. Just hanging local."

"He said he'd be by in the morning to say good-bye to you before school." She gave me a curious look as she started pulling groceries out of the bags and piling them up on the counter. "Are you and Peter okay?"

"M," I said, "D and I are totally cool."

"I'm glad," M said.

"How about you two?" I mean, if she could ask about my private life, couldn't I ask about hers?

M stopped suddenly, holding a jar of unsalted peanut butter in midair, and stared into space thoughtfully. Then she looked over at me and smiled. "I guess I will always love your father in some ways, Ran," she said slowly. "Mostly because when we were together, we made you, and whatever else, that was a great accomplishment. But, seeing him again, I realized, maybe for the first time, that we made the right decision when we got a divorce."

I nodded my head. I guess I kind of always knew that D and M wouldn't be getting back together. Sure, I'd hoped, but you can't fight reality. Not for long, anyway.

"How about Terry?" I asked.

"Whoa." M laughed. "Don't rush things. He's a nice guy, but it's a long way from being true love."

"Well, if it does turn out to be true love . . ." It was my turn to pause. "I guess that would be okay. There's just one thing, though."

"What's that?"

"We've gotta do something about those lame plaid shirts of his, M."

She ran over and gave me a big hug. Fortunately, I managed to stay cool this time. No tears, just a lot of smiles. I mean, I've got my reputation to think about, after all.

The next day I rolled out the door expecting to see D's limo. It wasn't there yet, but standing out on the sidewalk in the new snow were Katie and Sabs and Al.

"What's shakin'?" I asked.

"Nothing much," Katie answered.

It was totally obvious that they were all there because they thought I was still bummed about D. In case I didn't mention it before, my friends are the best.

Just then the limo pulled up, and D jumped out. "Ladies," he said, smiling his great smile. He came over and gave me a hug, which made Sabs go, "Aww."

"Christmas vacation, like we said?" D asked.

"Try and stop me," I answered. I could hear the car phone ringing.

"Telephone, Mr. Zak," Paul called out.

D looked at me and grinned. "Let 'em wait. I'm saying good-bye to my daughter."

In a million years I never thought I'd hear D say something like that. It almost made saying good-bye a little easier.

We watched the limo drive off, and for a couple of minutes nobody said a word. "Well, we'd better get going," Katie finally said quietly. "We don't want to be late."

"Yep," Al agreed. "Except there's just one little piece of business we have to take care of." She stooped down and picked up a big handful of fresh snow and began packing it into a ball. "Just one little piece of business," she said again with a wicked grin.

"Wait a minute, Al," Katie began. "That was

business. That was a job. It wasn't —"

The snowball hit her right in the face. "Okay, now we're even," Katie cried, spitting out the snow.

"Even?" Al asked. "Even? Do you think we're even, Randy?"

I shook my head regretfully. "I do seem to remember the number twenty-eight."

"Definitely, twenty-eight," Sabs agreed. At the same time Katie took off down the street with Al close behind her.

Katie is a pretty fast runner, but Sabs and I had a feeling that Al was going to find a way to give Katie those twenty-seven more snowballs.

Don't miss
GIRL TALK #23
HOUSE PARTY

"So, Eileen, can we go?" Jean-Paul asked my mom after the salad had been served.

"I don't know. I'm still worried about the children," Mom said, giving Emily, Michel, and me a concerned look.

I didn't have a clue to what they were talking about. Apparently, neither did Michel and Emily.

"Go where?" Michel wanted to know.

Jean-Paul looked at Mom expectantly. "I would like to take your mother away for a few days, but —"

"Mother, I am sixteen years old," Emily interrupted. "That's old enough to take care of myself and Katie and Michel. "I've been baby-sitting for other people since I was twelve!"

Mom didn't look convinced, though. "Emily, baby-sitting for a few hours is very different from being left alone for days while your parents are out of the country," she said.

"Out of the country!" I exclaimed. "Where are you going?" Mom and Jean-Paul had just gotten back from their honeymoon in France less than two months ago. Going someplace far away again so soon seemed pretty extreme.

Jean-Paul's dark eyes sparkled as he smiled at me. "It's only Bermuda, Katie," he said calmly. "Just a few hours away by plane."

Even though Jean-Paul was talking to me, I had the feeling he was trying to convince Mom, too. "We can leave Thursday and be home Sunday. Besides, Mrs. Smith will be here until after dinner every day we're gone."

"But Mr. O'Reilly will be away, too," Mom said worriedly.

"Eileen, it's only for three nights. We have a state-of-the-art alarm system and very responsible children," Jean-Paul insisted. "Besides, how often can you and I get away from work at the same time?"

I glanced at Michel, who looked excited about the idea of being on our own for a whole long weekend. Next to him, Emily looked hurt and angry. "Mother, if you don't trust me to run this house . . ." Her voice trailed off into a furious huff.

Actually, I could understand Mom's point of view. After all, we had never been left alone overnight before, and our big new house still felt a little strange and scary at night.

"Emily is right, Eileen," Jean-Paul said. "She is perfectly capable of being in charge of the house when Mrs. Smith and Cook are not here."

Emily got a smug, satisfied look on her face. Suddenly I had a bad feeling that if Mom did decide Emily could be in charge, Emily would act like some kind of crazed army general or something. "Why should Emily get to be in charge just because she's the oldest?" I asked. "I can take care of things just as well as she can."

"Me too," Michel chimed in.

"Thirteen is just too young," Mom said firmly.

"Mom, I can cook for the children on Sunday," Emily said in her most mature voice. Then she smiled sweetly at Michel and me.

I looked suspiciously at her. Somehow, in the last few minutes, Emily had gone from being *one* of the children to being *in control* of the children. Suddenly I could see that living with Emily while Mom and Jean-Paul were away was going to be anything but fun!

TALK BACK!
TELL US WHAT YOU THINK ABOUT
GIRL TALK BOOKS

Name _____

Address _____

City _____ State _____ Zip_____

Birthday _____ Mo._____ Year _____

Telephone Number (____) _____

1) Did you like this GIRL TALK book?

Check one: YES_____NO_____

2) Would you buy another GIRL TALK book?

Check one: YES_____NO_____

If you like GIRL TALK books, please answer questions 3–5; otherwise, go directly to question 6.

3) What do you like most about GIRL TALK books?

Check one: Characters_____Situations_____
         Telephone Talk_____Other_____

4) Who is your favorite GIRL TALK character?

Check one: Sabrina_____ Katie_____ Randy_____
Allison_____ Stacy_____ Other (give name)_____

5) Who is your *least* favorite character?

_____

6) Where did you buy this GIRL TALK book?

Check one: Bookstore____Toy store____Discount store_____

Grocery store___Supermarket___Other (give name)_____

Please turn over to continue survey.

7) How many GIRL TALK books have you read?

Check one: 0_____ 1 to 2_____ 3 to 4_____ 5 or more_____

8) In what type of store would you look for GIRL TALK books?

Bookstore_____ Toy store_____ Discount store_____

Grocery store_____ Supermarket_____ Other (give name)_____

9) Which type of store would you visit most often if you wanted to buy a GIRL TALK book?

Check *only* one: Bookstore_____ Toy store_____

Discount store_____ Grocery store_____ Supermarket_____

Other (give name)_____

10) How many books do you read in a month?

Check one: 0_____ 1 to 2_____ 3 to 4_____ 5 or more_____

11) Do you read any of these books?

Check those you have read:

The Baby-sitters Club_____ Nancy Drew_____

Pen Pals_____ Sweet Valley High_____

Sweet Valley Twins_____ Gymnasts_____

12) Where do you shop most often to buy these books?

Check one: Bookstore_____ Toy store_____

Discount store_____ Grocery store_____ Supermarket_____

Other (give name)_____

13) What other kinds of books do you read most often?

_____

14) What would you like to read more about in GIRL TALK?

_____

_____

Send completed form to :
GIRL TALK Survey, Western Publishing Company, Inc.
1220 Mound Avenue, Mail Station #85
Racine, Wisconsin 53404

LOOK FOR THE AWESOME GIRL TALK BOOKS
IN A STORE NEAR YOU!

MORE GIRL TALK TITLES TO LOOK FOR

Nonfiction
ASK ALLIE 101 answers to your questions about boys, friends, family, and school!

YOUR PERSONALITY QUIZ Fun, easy quizzes to help you discover the real you!

BOYTALK: HOW TO TALK TO YOUR FAVORITE GUY